THE PROTECTOR

Also by Shelley Shepard Gray

THE PROTECTOR

Families of Honor, Book Two

SHELLEY SHEPARD GRAY

**Doubleday Large Print
Home Library Edition**

AVON
INSPIRE

An Imprint of HarperCollins*Publishers*

This book is dedicated with much appreciation to librarians. Thank you for what you do. For people like me, who love to read, a world without a library would be a very lonely place.

This Large Print Edition, prepared especially for Doubleday Large Print Home Library, contains the complete, unabridged text of the original Publisher's Edition.

ISBN 978-1-61129-604-4

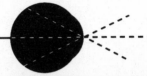

**This Large Print Book carries the
Seal of Approval of N.A.V.H.**

Now faith is being sure of what we hope for and certain of what we do not see.

~Hebrews 11:1 (NIV)

Share your joys with others. It takes two to be glad.

~Amish Proverb

Prologue

Nine years ago

"Come on, Ella," Corrine said, grabbing her mitten-covered hand. "If you walk much slower, we're going to be the last to arrive."

"That wouldn't be a bad thing," Ella murmured, though she clasped Corinne's hand and obediently followed her friend down the rocky incline toward Loyal Weaver's house. "Maybe we don't even need to go?"

Corrine looked at her like she'd just sprouted two heads. "Of course we do! Loyal invited everyone over for his birthday. It would be rude not to show up."

Ella pushed the center of her glasses back up on the bridge of her nose and picked up her pace. "Do you really think he meant everyone?" she asked uncertainly. "Maybe he didn't really mean that."

After all, through all their years together in school, Loyal had never gone out of his way to be her friend.

"Of course he did." Corrine squeezed her hand. "Come on, Ella, don't be so worried. It will be fun. You need to relax and smile more."

The Weavers' house was now in view, its white two-story frame looking tall and majestic on the hill in front of them. Scattered across the snowy front lawn were dozens of kids. It looked like Corrine had been exactly right. No one from their school had decided to miss the party.

But that was how it was with Loyal Weaver, she mused. He was the most handsome boy in her grade—maybe even in their school. But what was even more special than his looks was his attitude. Loyal was perpetually happy and chatty. He befriended everyone. It was rare to see him ever standing by himself.

Unlike her.

That had to be what happened when you were an only child, Ella mused. Her parents were naturally reticent and quiet. She was, too. But added to that was the feeling that she was never going to completely fit in like everyone else did. She wasn't super slim. She had glasses. And she had plain-old brown hair and brown eyes. In short, she was the complete opposite of smiling, golden-haired, blue-eyed Loyal Weaver.

Perhaps that was why she seemed to be the only person in their schoolhouse who didn't jump at the opportunity to visit him. They had nothing to say to each other.

"Oh, there's Paul! And Mattie! And Peter, too." Dropping Ella's hand, Corrine quickened her pace. "Do you think Peter will want to talk to me today?"

"I'm sure he will." Corrine was pretty and sweet and had her own share of admirers. Ella smiled. "I bet he'll walk up to you first thing."

"Maybe." Raising her voice, she called out, "Hi, everyone. Sorry we're late. Have we missed much?"

Mattie ran up to meet them, followed by Peter and Loyal and four others.

"All you've missed is Mrs. Weaver passing out hot cider and cookies."

"Oh, I'm sorry about that," Corrine smiled at Loyal. "Your *mamm* is a wonderful-*gut* cook."

"There's plenty of treats inside, Corrine," Loyal said. "Go on inside and help yourself." He grinned. "But first, I'm afraid you're gonna have to get by Peter. He's been standing here like an oak, waiting for you to appear."

The other kids laughed. Beside her Corrine blushed, then was wrapped up in the circle of the group, everyone walking in unison to the house.

Ella slowed. Not a person had acknowledged her. Or said hello. Or was even waiting on her. As usual, it was like she'd never even existed.

Suddenly, she knew she couldn't do it. She couldn't walk into the Weaver's home and sip cider and pretend everyone there wasn't ignoring her. She didn't want to stand off to the side, smiling awkwardly, hoping no one would notice how she didn't have her own group of friends.

But most of all, she didn't want to look at Loyal Weaver and chance that he'd see her watching him. Thinking how cute he was, how lucky the girl he chose to court would be. Even after all this time, it didn't even seem like he knew she existed.

She stopped, half waited for someone to call her name. Then, realized she was standing there by herself. Forgotten again.

There was only one thing to do. Ella Hostetler turned around and walked away.

Chapter 1

No matter how hard she tried, Ella Hostetler found it almost impossible to look away from the white canvas tent that covered the majority of her front yard.

She swallowed. Oh, it wasn't even *her* yard anymore. It, along with the house, barn, and most of the possessions inside, belonged to other people.

Now she had practically nothing.

"Ella, please don't stand and stare any longer. Watching you makes my heart break," Corrine said, her voice turning more troubled by the second. "*Ach*, but I knew I should have made you come over to my house today."

Corrine was a good friend. Her best friend in the world, next to Dorothy. But even good friends couldn't make difficult things go away. "I had to be here," Ella said. "Someone had to stay in case anyone bidding had a question." She tried to smile. "And it's not like there was anyone else to take my place."

Pure dismay entered Corrine's eyes. "Oh, but you've had such a time of it. First your father passed away, then you had to nurse your mother before she passed on, too—all while taking care of the house. All by yourself."

"I *am* an only child, Corrine."

"I know. But sometimes, I just feel so bad for you, having to sell everything."

Privately, Ella felt bad for herself, too. But hearing the doom and gloom in her girlfriend's voice pushed her to try to sound positive. "It will be a relief to not have so much to take care of," Ella said, almost believing it to be true. "And the money earned today will guarantee my future."

"Oh, Ella. You sound like you will never marry. You will."

"Maybe. Or maybe not. Perhaps I'll just be like Dorothy. She seems to be doing fine on her own."

Something flickered in her best friend's eyes. Was it distaste? Or distrust? "You are not like Dorothy. I've never met a crustier woman."

"She's not so bad."

"She's difficult and bitter. I wish you could have found a different person to move next to."

"The other half of her duplex was empty. Plus, she's excited for me to live there. We're going to work together at the library, you know."

"I know." Corrine pursed her lips. "I just can't help but feel that you're about to lock yourself away from everyone all over again, Ella. You should be making plans to see more people. To laugh a little. Not work and live next to Dorothy Zook."

A burst of the auctioneer's gavel sang through the air, preventing Ella from responding.

Casting another worried look her way, Corrine looped her arm through Ella's and pulled. "Come on. Let's go sit down."

Though Ella let herself be led away from

the crowd, she couldn't help but look over her shoulder. She could feel the knot in her throat expanding, making it almost too hard to continue talking. "I . . . had no idea I had so many things."

"We all have more than we need, *jah*?"

Ella flinched. Corrine's words were true . . . to a point. She'd known auctioning off her family's farm would be difficult. But this was so much more than that.

First her land and the buildings on it had been bought. And now so many others were picking and choosing through what remained of her parents' lives . . . putting a value on items that to her mother had been priceless.

Her feet slowed as she again couldn't resist looking over her shoulder. Against her will, tears sprang to her eyes as she watched the auctioneer point to her mother's pie safe.

Corrine paused, too. Bit her lip as he called out a price. "Ella, what is important are the memories. That is what everyone says."

"I know," she murmured, turning away. This was their way, to auction off things of the dead; she did understand the meaning behind it. And the far more practical reasoning: she was not going to need most of these items when she lived in town.

But if only memories were what counted, why was everyone else so eager to snatch up *her* things, *her* memories? And why did it hurt so much to watch them do it?

Corrine interrupted her thoughts. "Like I said, it has to be almost over. After all, Loyal Weaver bought most everything when he bought the land."

"Yes, he did." Nearly everything that had been her parents' was his now. To her dismay, he'd even bought a lot of the furniture. And her horse and buggy.

One day she would surely be thankful for the money in her bank account instead of her mare's sweet disposition. One day.

Picking up the pace, they moved farther from the tent—and away from the line of horses and buggies and *Englischers'* cars and trucks.

Away from the life Ella had always known.

They stopped in front of a finely carved bench. Made of weathered oak, the grain had long since been worn to a buttery smooth surface. There was a slight indention near the back, and a nick on the seat where Ella's father had once foolishly decided to test out his new whittling knife.

"Is right here okay?" Corrine asked.

"It is fine." Yes, it was almost far enough away. As she scanned the crowd through her glasses, most everyone became a blur. And then she saw Loyal Weaver. The man she'd always been aware of, but who had never noticed her. The man who with one purchase had changed her life.

Though it wasn't entirely fair, Ella focused all her pain on him. He was the one who'd been the first to arrive. Who had bid on her things with a gleam in his eye. Who had so much money that he'd paid cash for the land.

Just as if he bought other people's lives all the time.

"I've always liked this bench, Ella," Corrine murmured, claiming her attention again. "Remember how our legs used to swing when we sat here?"

"I remember." The worn bench had many special memories. It had been her grandmother's favorite place to sit on spring mornings; and her mother liked to sit and watch the geese fly south for the winter every October.

Ella herself had perched impatiently on it when she'd been looking for the English school bus to stop and pick her up.

And now it was Loyal Weaver's. And he most likely didn't even appreciate a bit of what he had.

When the auction was over and the majority of the crowd dispersed, Loyal bit his lip as he watched his older brother Calvin walk through the ancient barn. He touched the walls and the wooden stalls with his fingertips, but seemed to catch hold of every flaw in the structure, every crack in the wood with his eyes. The longer Calvin walked, the deeper his scowl.

After they'd made their way past the stalls and into a pair of rundown, musty tack rooms, Calvin stopped.

"Well?" Loyal asked. There was no sense in beating around the bush. His oldest brother was nothing if not honest. "What do you think?"

"I think it's terrible."

"Really?" He'd expected some criticism but not this blunt statement.

"Loyal, it boggles my mind why you

bought this place. I don't want to offend, but, really, there's no other way to say it. This place is fallin' apart. Whatever the termites haven't gotten, a good, strong wind will surely blow over."

So much for Calvin not wanting to offend! "This barn ain't so bad."

"It's not so good." After looking around again, Calvin strode out of the tack room. "It's so dark and cramped in there. Why, I doubt it's been cleaned out good in ten years." He shuddered. "Being in there makes me think of rats."

"I didn't see more than two," Loyal said dryly.

"I'm not laughing, *bruder*." Crossing the dusty, bug-infested ground, Calvin knocked on the wood of one of the stalls. "My word. This here wood sounds completely rotten."

That would be because it most likely was. "It only needs a little bit of work."

"For every day, the rest of your life." His brother pursed his lips, then finally sighed. "I just don't understand why you chose *this* place, and why now. I know you've been wanting to have a place of your own, but I think you were too hasty. Everything here—the barn, the house, even the land—has been neglected for far too long."

"It has promise." Irritation coursed through him as he crossed the expanse to where his brother stood tapping the toe of his boot like he had somewhere else he'd rather be. "I'm not afraid of hard work, you know." When Calvin's eyes flashed, Loyal braced himself for the next barrage of criticism that was sure to come. "What has you so upset? Are you upset about the money I spent? We agreed it was mine to use how I chose."

"Of course it was your money. And it's not that."

"Then what?" Loyal eyed Calvin, wondering what was going through his brain. Now that he was happily married, had he become complacent? Had he forgotten what it was like to want something of your very own to treasure? To make a mark on?

His brother didn't disappoint. "I know you're not afraid of hard work. And I understand your need to carve out a place all your own. But this place is no good. The barn is in disrepair, the fields are poorly maintained, and that house . . ." He shook his head. "That house is almost worthless. There's nothing of value there."

Loyal thought differently. The Hostetlers' land was on fertile soil and had the makings of a mighty nice farm, indeed. All it had lacked were funds and muscle to make repairs and improvements. He had plenty of both.

The former owners had had neither.

For months, rumors had been circulating that Ella would sell the place as soon as her mother went to heaven. Three months ago, she passed on. Ella had kept her promise, and today an auction was held for what remained.

Now he was finally able to step out of his older brother's shadow.

Almost against his will, Loyal looked across the yard to a lone bench on the driveway. There sat Ella Hostetler. *Plain Ella*, they'd all called her when they were children.

Ella turned her head as if she'd felt his gaze, or heard his thoughts. She peered right back at him.

Loyal felt his cheeks flush. "I think I should go speak to Ella."

Calvin grabbed his arm. "Don't."

"I have to, Calvin. She's hurting."

"Of course she is. She just sold off everything she could."

Guilt washed over him. "To me."

"And others." Lowering his voice, Calvin said earnestly, "Ella's disappointment is not your fault. If you didn't spend your hard-earned money on this . . ." He looked around distastefully. "This *place*, someone else would have."

Loyal jerked his arm away. Why did his older brother never cease to be the voice of authority on every single subject? "You're making perfect sense, but I have to try to make things better between Ella and me."

"There is nothing you could say to make things right. At least not today."

"All I'm going to do is tell her I understand—"

"You understand what? That you've now given her the money she needed to move on with her life?" Calvin lowered her voice. "Loyal, I do understand your motives, and I even understand Ella's pain. But it's not like she's been a friend of ours. In school, she never played with the rest of us; she always had her head in a book. And since then, she's kept to herself."

Loyal had the sinking suspicion that she would have put a book away if kids had ever invited her to play. Unbidden, a memory rushed forward, of her showing up at his house for his birthday. He'd been so surprised to see her, he hadn't thought to greet her properly.

Later, he found out that she'd left, not even going inside, because he'd ignored her.

And that had shamed him.

"Let her be," Calvin whispered again. "If anything, your presence will embarrass her. The folks who haven't left yet will watch. And then they'll talk. It's better just to keep your distance."

What his brother said made sense. He turned away and went back to inspecting the stalls.

But every so often, Loyal still felt Ella's gaze on him.

And still felt her pain.

Chapter 2

As the horse languidly clopped along over the concrete, hot summer air blew into the buggy. The slight breeze offered Ella a momentary respite from the humidity.

Not enough for any true relief, though. The back of Ella's neck was damp with perspiration, and she felt as if every muscle in her body was sore. That had to be the by-product of a week's worth of worry and stress.

Ella was glad that Corrine's husband and brother had helped move her things into her new apartment the day before. Though she had lots of boxes to unpack and regular chores to look forward to, nothing sounded as good as a cool shower, a few minutes sipping chamomile tea, and a few precious moments to read a chapter of her newest book.

However, Corrine didn't see things that way. For the majority of the journey to her new home, her girlfriend had fretted. "I do wish you'd reconsider my invitation," she said yet again.

And yet again, Ella deflected her worries. "All I want to do is relax, Corry. I can do that best on my own."

"Oh, I know you're tired. And I know you only want to sip tea and read."

Ella caught the slight edge of sarcasm. "It's what I like to do."

"I know. But we have tea at our house. And if you were there, Peter and I could visit with you, too."

"We're visiting now," Ella said gently. What she wanted to add was that she yearned for peace and quiet. Not conversation.

Corrine darted an exasperated glance her way. "I just hate to think of you spending your first night away from the farm in an *apartment.*"

Ella couldn't help but notice that every time Corrine said "apartment," she winced. "It's actually more than just an apartment, you know. It's half a duplex. And it's my new home. I'll be fine."

"That's not the same as being comfortable. I have the guest bedroom all ready for you."

"I thank you, but I won't be needin' it," Ella said as Corrine pulled her horse to a stop in front of a two-story clapboard home on the main road through Jacob's Crossing. "I'll be fine here. Besides, I won't be alone. Dorothy will be on the other side."

Corrine nibbled her bottom lip as she looked at the duplex. "I wish you wouldn't have rushed to take Dorothy up on her offer of lodging. Living here seems like a punishment."

It was, indeed, a far cry from the farm where she'd grown up. Instead of acres of wildflowers, gardens, and woods, she now had a small backyard and nary a tree in sight. Instead of having a large, comfortable farmhouse to move around in, she was going to be cramped in half of a house. But it would be fine. It had to be. "It's certainly no punishment."

She scampered out, thankful for their buggies' lack of doors. Ella was sure she would fairly scream if things dragged on much longer.

With a sigh, Corrine picked up the reins. "All right. I can see you're anxious to leave. I'm going to check on you tomorrow. If you get scared tonight, living in the middle of town like this, you can come to our house."

Ella held back a smile. Corrine really did have a heart of gold. "I won't be scared. Actually, I'm so exhausted, the only thing I will likely be doing is closing my eyes. And I can't think of a better thing to do than sleep in my own bed."

Looking over her carefully, Corrine finally smiled. "I suppose you're right. *Gut nacht,* Ella. Sleep well."

"*Gut nacht,* to you, too," she said, then got out her last suitcase and waved her sweet friend on. "And thank you. You made today bearable."

The moment Corrine's buggy moved on, Dorothy stepped out of her front door. "You are finally here!" Coming forward, she wrapped Ella in a generous hug. "*Wilkum!* I thought you'd never arrive."

As Ella tiredly curved her arms around

Dorothy's generous girth, she fought to keep a smile on her lips. "What a nice welcome. *Danke!* I didn't expect to see you until tomorrow at work."

"We're neighbors now. I think we'll see each other all the time." An edge entered her tone as she stepped back and looked Ella over. "Besides, I've been waiting for hours, practically going blind, staring out the window. It's after eight o'clock. What took you so long?"

A twinge of alarm flashed through Ella. Why was Dorothy acting so possessive? "I was at the auction, of course."

"Couldn't you leave it?"

"I didn't want to."

"But the people who ran the sale didn't need you to sit there and watch . . . did they?"

"No," Ella conceded. "But still, I couldn't leave, not if people had questions."

Dorothy's piercing light gray eyes seemed to weigh her answer and find it wanting. "Is that right? When I stopped by the auction earlier today, I didn't even see you. I looked all over the area and in the tent."

"I'm sorry I missed you. I wasn't with the people buying things. I tried to stay out of the way." Ella fought back the urge to apologize further. She hadn't done anything wrong, but Dorothy was looking at her as if she had. "Why were you there?"

"I came to shop of course."

"You went to purchase items?" Ella knew her voice had turned husky, but she didn't care.

"Oh, *jah*," Dorothy said in that matter-of-fact way of hers. Just like they were talking about new fabrics for sale at the Wal-Mart in Middlefield. "There were some mighty good prices to be found. Bargains, they were."

Bargains on her family's possessions. "I see . . ."

Dorothy prattled on. "I didn't stay long. I left as soon as I bought a few things."

Perhaps she was simply tired, but the whole conversation was making her uneasy. Though she knew she was being silly, Ella felt betrayed. Somehow she'd imagined Dorothy would feel as strange about the sale as Corrine did. Ella knew she would herself, if the situations were reversed. With a hint of reluctance, she asked, "What did you buy?"

"Your mother's ceramic nesting bowls.

And a pretty basket. You know the one that was always in your front hall?"

"I know it." Her heart wrenched for at least the hundredth time that day as she recalled how her mother had filled that basket with pairs of brightly colored mittens in the winter and freshly clipped daisies in the summer.

"Well, I've always admired that basket, so I took the opportunity to purchase it." Looking down at Ella, Dorothy added, "A woman living on her own needs to learn to see to her needs, *jah*? That is something I'm sure you'll learn over the years."

Over the years?

It took everything Ella had to school her features into something completely blank. Dorothy made it sound like Ella would be living on her own forever. Though she didn't have any prospects, she'd never given up the hope that she'd be able to create a family of her own one day.

In addition, Dorothy sounded so pleased about the bargains she found. Did she not understand that those bargains had once been a part of Ella's life?

Silence pulled between them, becoming uncomfortable.

Dorothy cleared her throat. "This is where you tell me thank you, Ella."

"Pardon me?"

"I helped your finances," she prodded as she folded her arms across her chest, looking for a moment like an angry bull. "I came to your auction and paid my hard-earned money for old belongings of yours."

"Danke," Ella said dutifully, but in truth, she felt more confused than ever. Was that really what everyone who had visited the auction had thought? That she was someone to be pitied . . . and that she now owed them her gratitude?

It was a curious—and uncomfortable— feeling to be in debt to someone for buying her family's possessions. More than ever, Ella desperately needed some time alone. "I don't want to be rude, but I'm afraid I just can't talk right now. I really am *schlaeferich.*" Actually, she felt more exhausted than sleepy.

"You're sleepy? Are you sure? I was going to give you a tour of your new home."

At this moment? When it was so obvious that she could barely string two sentences together? "There's no need—"

"I think so. I think there's every need. I

wanted to be sure you understand how to work everything. And to show you that all the appliances and faucets are in proper working order. It is as it should be."

Again, there was an unexpected note of steel in Dorothy's tone, like she was almost eager for an argument. Or eager to push and push.

It was too much for Ella to take. "Everything was fine yesterday."

"Yes, but we need to make sure there are no surprises, right? If something is wrong, then I could be blamed. For all purposes, I am your landlady now."

"You are, but we're still *freinds*. Of course I wouldn't blame you, Dorothy."

"We are, but even friends can be cruel to each other." As that phrase lingered, Dorothy flashed a smile. "But I'm being silly, of course. We could never be like that, could we?"

Ella shook her head slowly. A slow, sinking feeling settled in her stomach as they walked down the sidewalk to the front entrance.

Though moving from her farm to a tiny apartment had been one of the hardest things she'd ever done, in the back of her mind, Ella had hoped that there would be something positive that would come from it. That, in the end, she would now have the opportunity to make more friends. Needless to say, it had been a long, hard year caring for her mother, doing her best to keep up with the farm . . . and then giving it all away.

As they climbed up the three stairs that led to the front door, one of the steps creaked under Ella's weight.

Immediately, Dorothy bent and inspected the stair. Then she lifted her face to Ella's. "I don't see any loose nails. Do you?"

Ella glanced at the step halfheartedly. The light was too dim to see much, and at the moment, she could care less about loose nails.

All she ached to do was sleep. "I think it is fine," she murmured.

"All right, then." Dorothy straightened. With her own key, she unlocked Ella's door.

That took her by surprise. "I didn't realize you had your own key to my apartment."

"Well, of course I do. I'm the owner, after all."

But that still didn't seem right. "But I'm paying you rent. I wouldn't feel comfortable if you used your key to come inside without me knowing." As a matter of fact, she wasn't terribly comfortable with the ease in which Dorothy was letting herself into her place now.

"Ella, I'm not going to want to spy on you."

The hint of unease became a full-fledged knot of worry. Dorothy seemed angry, and more than a little secretive.

Ella now wondered what other secrets Dorothy kept hidden away.

"I know you won't spy," Ella said quickly. "It's just that . . . well, I'm used to living on my own. That farm was a big place, you know. I'm used to being by myself."

"Now you won't have to. Soon, we'll do everything together and you won't ever have to be lonely again," Dorothy said with a hint of iron in her voice. "Why, years from now, I bet we'll laugh about this con-versation. *Years from now*, we'll forget what it was like, ever living apart!"

There was that reminder once again. *Years from now.*

As if Ella's life was pretty much over, that she now had nothing to look forward to except life in half a duplex next to another old maid.

Those things had never been in Ella's dreams. Unbidden, Corrine's warnings rang in her ears. Had Corrine been right? Had she been too hasty in making her future plans?

As she followed Dorothy into her apartment and listened to Dorothy talk about the water pressure and the best way to the clean the linoleum floor, Ella's sense of unease heightened. Though nothing her friend was saying was quite wrong, it didn't feel quite right, either.

Chapter 3

Mattie Lapp had survived breast cancer, surgery, and four terrible rounds of chemotherapy. Through it all, she'd been so sick she could hardly walk, and so weak she feared she'd ever be able to do anything by herself ever again.

She'd comforted a weepy mother and smiled bravely for the numbers of people who cooked and prayed for her.

Usually, she liked to think of herself as rather tough. She liked to think of herself as a survivor.

Except for right at that moment. At the moment, she felt weak and scared and completely alone. A giant, furry spider lurking behind a basket did that to her. *"Ach!"* she cried as the beast seemed to double in size right before her eyes. "Oh! Why are you here?"

In response, the spider scurried toward her.

"Oh! *Ach!*" she cried out again, feeling as irritated by the situation as she was scared of the small insect—and its friends, who were surely hiding.

Why in the world did it have to appear right now? When she was all alone? And just after she'd washed the floors, too.

Before her eyes, the spider's body continued to balloon in size. Now it was at least as big as a silver dollar.

She tried to recall what she'd learned of spiders. Was it pregnant? Carrying around an egg sack? The very idea of it made her squirm. Though Mattie knew she was overreacting, she darted out the kitchen door to the safety of her front porch.

"Whoa, there, Mattie." Two solid hands reached out, holding her securely by the shoulders.

She knew that grip! With a grateful sigh, she turned in relief. "Oh, Graham! Graham, thank goodness you're here. I need your help."

"You do, hmm?" He smiled slowly as he leisurely eyed her from top to bottom. She felt him pause on the babylike fuzz on her head, and then on her bare toes curling on the wood floor planks.

Still holding her shoulders, he asked, "Do I even want to know what's got you into such a state?"

As usual, he knew exactly what to say to get her riled up. "You never fail to make me sound like I'm *shvach*."

"I don't think you're *shvach* at all. Well . . . perhaps just a little bit weak."

"Graham!"

He quirked an eyebrow. "Mattie, you are squealing and carrying on something awful. And on your front porch, no less."

"I don't squeal."

Eyes still twinkling, he said, too patiently, "Forgive me. I misspoke. You are never weak and you never squeal."

"Graham . . ."

He continued, ignoring her warning. "Oh, *jah*. You, Mattie Lapp, are always perfect." One eyebrow rose. "Except, perhaps, at this very moment?"

She felt her cheeks heat. "I have a good reason."

"Which is?"

She exhaled. "I saw a spider." Of course, even as she said the words, Mattie knew she sounded a bit silly.

"Did you, now?" He had the nerve to nod, like what she was saying made perfect sense. "I see. So when you saw the thing, you decided to run out here?"

Oh, she hated it when he sounded so sure and full of himself! "It's big, Graham. Terribly big. The biggest one I've ever seen." And because she was willing to be called weak and helpless and silly right at this moment she added, "And you need to go inside and kill it."

"It looks like I came at just the right time. You were in need of a real man." He flexed one arm. Even through the loose cotton, his bicep was pronounced.

"I'm not kidding, Graham. It's a horrible, terribly big spider."

"It won't be too big for me," he bragged. He waved a hand in front of her. "Show me where this creature is."

Pointing through the screen, she said, "It's in there. You can't miss it." There was no way she was going to be in the same room with it again. "On the kitchen floor."

"Mattie," he said with exaggerated patience, "come inside with me."

"I'd rather not."

"Fine." He opened up the door.

"Wait! You don't want to go in unarmed," she cried while grabbing the broom standing against the wall and handing it to him, saying, "You're going to need this. Or perhaps even a shovel."

He had the nerve to roll his eyes. "Yes, like your mother would appreciate a dirty shovel on her floor." Looking around, he picked up a section of newspaper from the square wooden box by the front door. "This will do nicely."

"I doubt it." She *so* doubted it, she kept right where she was. Where it was safe.

"If we wait much longer, it will go somewhere else."

That was all she needed to push open the door and press her hand to his shoulder blade, guiding him inside.

She stayed a good two feet behind.

"Mattie? You are being too silly. You need to show me where it is."

"There." She peeked around him and

saw the villain resting in front of the leg of her mother's wooden chopping block. "There!"

"Where?" A split second later, he stepped back in alarm, his eyes wide. "Oh! Watch out! The thing just jumped."

Mattie would have grinned if she wasn't so scared. However, his fright made her braver. Little by little, she scooted closer. "I told you. It's enormous."

In front of her, Graham's muscles tensed. She watched him hesitate, then roll up the latest edition of the *Budget* into a paper sword.

"My *daed* isn't going to like you using that."

"He's going to like living with this . . . *beast* even less. Watch out now." Like a fencer, he charged the spider. The spider, of course, scurried out of the way.

Graham straightened, obviously flummoxed. "Where did it go?"

"There!" Mattie pointed to the top of the butcher block.

Graham attacked again. *Splat!* went the paper. But the spider was quicker. It darted out and literally hopped three inches.

"Ach!" Mattie screamed again, unable

to help herself. When Graham grunted, slammed down the newspaper, and missed, she scanned the table and found it next to her mother's glass vase filled with flowers. "There it is!" she said, pointing.

Down went the newspaper.

With a resounding crash, the vase broke, leaving a trail of broken glass and water in its wake.

But Graham beamed triumphantly. "I got it!"

Mattie peeked around his shoulder and wrinkled her nose. "You got it, all right. But—oh, what a mess. The spider is on the paper, on the butcher block, too. Graham. Did you really have to put quite so much force behind your attack?"

"I'm afraid I did, Mattie. See, I hardly know my own strength."

"Oh, brother."

Looking almost contrite, he said, "I am sorry about the vase. I thought my aim was a bit better."

"It wasn't," she retorted just as her mother came running in.

"What in the world is going on? I heard you carrying on when I was parking the buggy," she explained, looking at the both

of them like they were mischievous schoolchildren.

Just like she used to do when they *were*
mischievous schoolchildren.

"Oh, nothing, Mamm. Graham was just
killing a spider for me."

"Only one?" She looked from one to the
other and shook her head. "It sounded like
you were waging war on a colony of in-
truders, Graham."

"It was mighty big," Graham said.

Her mother frowned. "You two broke my
vase."

"It couldn't be helped, Mamm," Mattie
replied. "Believe me, you'd rather have the
spider gone than a vase in perfect condi-
tion."

"I would have rather had both." Looking
from one to the other, her mother sighed.
"Graham, are you sure you killed it, at
least?"

"Positive." Looking helpful, he lifted up
the paper to show her the remains. "I am
sorry about the mess, but it truly was a
verra big intruder."

Grabbing a handful of paper towels,
Mattie said, "I'll clean it up."

Again looking back and forth at them,

her mother's scowl slowly faded away into a full-fledged grin. "Oh, you two. Together, you really are a pair of trouble. Just like when you were small. Some things never change, hmm?"

She snatched the paper towels from Mattie's hands. "For now, I think it would be best if I did the cleaning. Mattie, you may go out and clip more flowers for me from the garden. Graham, you may help her carry them."

"*Danke,* Mamm." Sharing a mischievous look with Graham, Mattie led the way outside. "I truly am grateful for your help with that spider, you know."

"I know."

"What brings you by here? Other than to kill giant bugs?"

"Actually, I came for a reason. I need some advice," he said, taking the wicker basket from her hands and leading the way to her mother's flower garden.

"About what?"

"About Jenna Yoder."

"Jenna? What about her?"

Looking almost embarrassed, he mumbled, "I think she's pretty. I want to court her."

Pure dismay made her stop in her tracks. "When did this come about? I . . . I didn't know you were interested in courting anyone."

Once again, he looked at her like she was being particularly naïve. "Why wouldn't I want to be courtin'? Most everyone in our group of friends is paired off."

That was true. Everyone did seem to have someone. Some, like Lucy and Calvin, and Corrine, were already married. Others had just announced their engagement.

And still others were falling in love.

Everyone but her, of course. She'd been busy fighting cancer while others were kissing and flirting and planning their futures.

Graham swung the basket slightly. "So, what do you know about her? You two used to be friends in school, weren't ya?"

"We were." Thinking of her golden hair, greenish blue eyes, and perfect smile, Mattie struggled for something to say. "Jenna is a sweet girl."

"All girls are sweet," he said with a dismissive wave of his hand.

"No, they're not."

He sighed. "Mattie, help me out, please. What does Jenna like? What does she like to do? I want to take her on a drive on Saturday afternoon."

A pang of jealousy slid through her, as unwelcome as that spider had been. "She likes most anything, I imagine."

"That is no help. Tell me something useful."

No, she wasn't being any help at all, Mattie realized with some dismay. Why was she so jealous?

Graham certainly didn't deserve that. Thinking quickly, she said, "You know what? Jenna has always liked arts and crafts. She draws well, sews darling little animals for newborns, and has even designed quilts. I'm sure she would enjoy walking around the arts-and-crafts festival."

"The one on Chardon Square?"

She nodded. "There are a lot of exhibits there. You two will be able to walk around and look at all the displays. It will be a *gut* way to spend some time together."

"*Danke,* Mattie." Smiling, he said, "She sounds even better than I imagined. Not only is she mighty pretty, but she's talented, too."

"Yes, she's a wonder."

Luckily, Graham didn't catch her note of sarcasm. "When I see her tomorrow, I'm going to ask her to the fair."

She stopped in her tracks. "*Mariye?* Tomorrow?"

"Well, *jah*. I thought I'd stop by her family's produce market and ask her there."

"You're serious about her, aren't you?"

"I am. Well, I hope to be," he explained, looking boyish.

For some reason, she didn't care for that news at all. Until today, it had never occurred to her that one day Graham would court a woman and get married.

But that, of course, was no way to repay his friendship.

Not only did he kill bugs at a moment's notice, but he'd been with her through thick and thin. He'd held her when she'd been so sick with the chemotherapy treatments, and teased her when she'd first shaved her head.

No matter what, she needed to support him. Even if it made her slightly uncomfortable to imagine him charming some other girl.

Putting on her very best smile, Mattie

reached out and squeezed his shoulder. "I hope she says yes to the fair. And I hope you both have a wonderful-*gut* time. You deserve it."

Pressing his hand to hers lightly, he nodded. "*Danke,* Mattie."

Suddenly, it felt too awkward. She gracefully pulled away from his touch and clasped both hands in front of her. She tried to concentrate on the way the warm breeze felt as it slid under her *kapp* and caressed her almost bare head.

Pretended she didn't mind that she no longer had long, pretty hair like Jenna did.

Pretended that it didn't matter that no man in Jacob's Crossing was eager to take her for a buggy ride or for a walk around an arts-and-crafts fair.

She supposed things would just stay the same. But obviously, like the appearance of cancer, one just never knew what the future had in store.

Chapter 4

"You're an official landowner now, Loyal," John Weaver, his uncle, teased from the other side of the counter of his donut-and-coffee restaurant, The Kaffi Haus. "How does it feel?"

As several of the men in the restaurant looked on with amused smiles, Loyal shrugged. "For the most part, it feels pretty good."

"That's it?" John asked, his expression filled with surprise. "You are the nephew who has something to say about everything."

"Not really."

"No, I'm afraid I have to tell you differently. Even when you were small you were never satisfied with a simple 'pretty good' with anything. Always, you had to expound upon things. Two words were never enough."

His uncle's words embarrassed him. Made him think that perhaps he'd said too much too often. Or, perhaps he'd always liked the sound of his own voice? "Maybe I've grown up."

"Maybe." Uncle John looked at him intently—in the way he had of making Loyal feel, with just one look, that he knew his deepest feelings. "Are the bills and the obligations already weighing ya down?"

"Never. I can handle all of that with no problem."

"There's the Loyal Weaver I remember," Henry Miller said, making a small toast with his cup. "You always did have confidence to spare."

"Only a bit."

"It near drove your father to distraction when you were small," Henry said as he eyed him with a smile. "But then, you were also a great source of pride, too. He'd be proud of you."

"I hope so," Loyal said, feeling his heart expand in his chest. Sitting among his father's friends brought forth a fresh wave of nostalgia. Being the middle son had always made him feel like he was not quite old enough, that he would never measure up to either his father or Calvin.

But now, at this moment, it felt like he'd finally made a step forward into adulthood.

It felt momentous.

"Owning my own land feels like I expected," he said after taking another sip of coffee. "Well, it feels like what I'd hoped," he amended.

"You're going to do just fine. You've always had a way about you."

Actually, the whole situation felt far different than he'd anticipated. For most of his life, he'd yearned to step out of his father's and Calvin's shadows. He'd known the only way to do that was to go someplace where he could be in charge. For the last year, he'd been patiently waiting for some land to become available.

As soon as he'd learned Ella Hostetler was putting her land up for auction, he jumped at the chance. On paper, it had sounded like a wonderful-*gut* situation. The

Hostetler's land was close to his family's acreage. He would be nearby but also living a more independent lifestyle. In short, it would give him everything he'd always wanted.

He'd been able to get the land for a good price, too. His mother was happy. And his brothers, while not necessarily understanding of his excitement, were sure to come around.

After a few more minutes of ribbing, John said, "I haven't seen Ella lately, but I hope she is making her adjustment all right."

"I hope so as well."

Every time he thought about Ella, and the complete look of dismay he'd seen on her face during the auction, a shadow fell upon his mood. He'd convinced himself that he was giving her the opportunity to live a better life in Jacob's Crossing. Living in the middle of town instead of the outskirts gave her an opportunity to be around more people, to have her dream job of working in the library. After all, everyone knew she'd basically been by herself for the last year, caring for her mother as she had.

But she'd looked so devastated at the auction, Loyal felt as if he'd just done something terrible. He really should have ignored Calvin's advice and gone over to talk to her.

Mr. Schlabach looked him over. "What are you going to do first? Repair the barn or the house? I heard both need a lot of work."

"I hope to work on both at the same time. Both are usable, just in need of some elbow grease."

One eyebrow rose. "From several elbows." Looking at the other men at the breakfast bar, John said, "I am thinking next Saturday would be a wonderful-*gut* time to lend you a hand. What say you?"

"I'd say I'd be grateful for your hands. And elbows! *Danke.*"

"We're happy to help, aren't we, men?"

That, of course, brought along another round of teasing. Then, one by one, they got up and said goodbye. "Good luck to you," Henry said as he left the donut shop. "See you on Saturday."

Taking a tasty bite of his chocolate donut, Loyal waved him and the others off and noticed Ella leaving her house and walking down the sidewalk.

Her gray dress seemed looser than usual, her pace slow. Actually, her whole body looked tired and depressed.

Instantly, the guilt came back. No matter how hard he tried to pretend otherwise, he knew he was the cause of her pain.

There was no way he could stay seated as she walked by. What he needed to do was finally gather his courage and go say something to her. Even if she was mighty angry at him, it was the right thing to do.

It was surely what his father would have expected of him.

After a quick wave goodbye to Uncle John, he darted out of the shop and ran across the street. *"Ella?* Ella, hello!"

She stopped for him, but even he couldn't describe her expression as anything less than put-upon as he approached.

"Gut mariye, Loyal."

"Good morning to you." When she continued to look curiously at him through her glasses, the pretty little speech he'd planned to say went walking. "I was, uh, just having a donut. Want to join me?"

She froze, looking like he'd just sprouted feathers. "I already had breakfast today."

"Oh, I have, too. I ate early. Lucy's cooking for us now, and she makes a fine break-fast at five A.M." He closed his eyes as he realized he was rambling. "I'm, uh, just having a little snack. Would you care for one?"

"A snack?"

"Yes."

"Ah, *nee*. No, thank you."

Loyal supposed he didn't blame her. Never before had he gone out of his way to talk with her, not even when they were teenagers and both were at the same singings. Actually, he'd gone out of his way to ignore her.

Remembering how brash he'd been, he tried to connect with her again. "I didn't know if you'd had breakfast yet. It was just an idea." Still floundering—floundering terribly—he added, "I can't seem to stay away from the donuts."

Her gaze skimmed his face, then, to his surprise, a reluctant smile formed. "Obviously not." Pointing to the corner of her lips, she said, "You've got a bit of chocolate there."

"Do I?" Feeling like he'd lost all his manners, he wiped his face with the side of his hand. "I guess I should be more careful, hmm?"

"Perhaps." After another, almost-amused look his way, she started walking again.

He fell into step beside her. "So, where are you going this morning?"

"Work." Beneath the glasses, her brown eyes lit up. "Today is my first day of work at the library."

"Are you looking forward to it?"

"Oh, yes." Some of that light in her eyes seemed to travel to her cheeks, turning them rosy. The added color did wonderful things to her skin, making it seem almost translucent. All of a sudden, *Plain Ella* didn't look plain at all.

No. All of a sudden, she looked pretty and fresh—and younger, too.

With another almost-hesitant smile his way, she continued: "I've always loved the library. I feel blessed to work there now."

Something about the way she said it gave him pause. She really was looking forward to her job. "What will you do?"

"Oh, shelve books and check them out, I suppose." Darting a sideways glance his way, she smiled. "And do whatever else Ms. Donovan asks of me."

Her enthusiasm made him smile, both

at her and at himself. Selfishly, he'd been only thinking about how different her life was. And that she would be sad because of his part in it.

Sometimes his ego seemed too big for his head!

"I hope you have a good day," he finally murmured, though he ached to say so much more. He wanted to tell her how sorry he was that both her parents had gone to heaven.

And how bad he'd felt for her circumstances, having to work her land by herself for the last year. And that he was going to do his best by her property. How he would be a good protector of it.

But how could he put all that into words without seeming too full of himself?

"I hope you have a pleasant day as well." She took two steps, then looked his way again. Probably because he was still walking with her!

"Loyal . . . ah, I hope you won't take this the wrong way, but please don't feel guilty about the auction. Or my move."

Now he was completely embarrassed. He really should have said something earlier. "I don't," he fibbed. At her look of confusion, he amended his words. "Well, not too much."

"You shouldn't feel guilty at all. I'm the one who put it for sale. Not you."

"But I was anxious to have the land," he admitted, his cheeks heating.

To his amazement, she chuckled. "That's the way of auctions, don'tcha think? Someone has to buy what's offered."

"I suppose . . ."

"I just want you to know that, since someone had to buy my farm, I'm glad it was you."

"Really?" He couldn't have been more surprised. Or humbled.

"You care about the land."

She swallowed, finally losing some of that careful reserve he'd spied under her frames.

"And, um, you've always been a nice person."

He'd never imagined she'd thought about such things. Never imagined that she'd thought about him. Like that. Especially since he knew that he could've been a fair sight nicer.

"I will get used to living in town, and getting the chance to work at the library is nice. I couldn't work here if I was still on the farm."

"All right. But if there's a reason for you to come show me something at the farm, would you?'

"What could you possibly need?"

He started walking with her toward the library. "Well, I thought I might paint the walls in the house and refurbish the floor. What do you think of that idea? Have you ever painted it a color? Or was it always white inside?"

"It has always been white, but I have thought a pale gray or blue would look nice in the bedrooms," she said, surprising him. "The shade trees make things so cool in the afternoons, I thought a faint color would be pretty. You know, it might warm things up a bit."

Eager to talk with her a little bit longer, Loyal said, "Do you have a trick for the front door lock? It sticks."

"I don't think I locked the door much," she said after a moment's consideration. "But there is a trick. You have to pull in the knob sharply before you turn the handle."

"Pull in the knob, turn the handle. I'll do that."

Stopping in front of the library, she hugged her arms in front of her. "Well, I suppose I had best go in now. I don't want to be late for my first day of work."

"And I don't want to make you late. Hey, um, Ella?"

"Yes?"

"I just wanted you to know . . . I'm mighty glad we walked together."

She blinked behind her glasses, then smiled. The genuine expression lighting up her face and transforming her shy expression into something far different. She looked almost pretty. . . . No, she was pretty, he realized with a start.

"I am as well," she said, then turned and walked away.

As she went, he wondered when he would find an excuse to stop by to see her again.

Chapter 5

Little by little, John Weaver's rush of early-morning customers filtered out, ready to begin their days. They left the coffee shop almost empty except for a few tables of regulars.

And that, John had to admit, was the way he liked things.

Just four months ago, he moved back to Jacob's Crossing after spending twenty years in Indianapolis. In the city, he'd had a good job working for a tire distributor. He weighed and balanced tires, organized the warehouse, and eventually was in charge of inventory.

The men he worked with had been a good bunch. They'd joked and sweated and got dirty. Being covered in dust and grime was a given when a man lugged tires for hours each day. But during the last few years, John had known that he needed a break from this demanding, sometimes stressful job.

Then, in April, when his nephew Calvin had come for a visit with his little sister Katie in tow, John had taken their appearance as a sign from God. It was time to reacquaint himself with his roots. And his family.

In short, it was time to go home—even though this home had been no home to him in almost two decades.

However, that decision must have all been part of God's plan—because, in no time, he'd hit it off with Amos House, the longtime owner of the Kaffi Haus. It just so happened that Amos liked making donuts, not waiting on customers—the complete opposite of John. Amos also had an empty apartment on the second floor of the building. Almost too easily, John was living above the donut shop and was waiting on customers, becoming acquainted with everyone in the community. Fitting in.

And then he'd met Jayne Donovan. The librarian. Against his will, John still felt himself blush whenever he thought of the lady. In short, she was everything he'd ever dreamed of when he'd been seventeen and contemplating jumping the fence. Jayne had short dark-brown hair, a striking figure, and almost violet eyes. She was perpetually grinning and had a teasing, flirty personality that never failed to draw him close.

She was kind, too. Underneath all that vivaciousness was a good heart.

In many ways, John thought she was perfect for him. That was a bit of a shock— since he hadn't thought he'd ever longingly look at another woman after his wife, following just two years of marriage, divorced him.

John had been trying to remember how to ask Jayne, or any woman, out—it had been a long time since he'd dated—when still another woman came into his life.

Confusing him.

Mary Zehr was the exact opposite of Jayne. She was younger than Jayne's thirty-four years. Younger by at least three or four years. She was quiet, too. And pretty, though not striking like Jayne. No, there was a serene, almost angelic beauty to her pale green eyes and brown hair. She was slim and gentle. She was also a widow—and was raising a twelve-year-old boy by herself.

John didn't know much about children, perhaps suggesting that, as a single mom, he should have been scared off. But Mary was so loving with her son Abel that John couldn't help but be drawn to her.

Yes, he was drawn to Mary in an almost visceral way. His heart beat a little faster whenever she came to the store; he watched himself around her, wanted to be gentle with her. Wanted to earn her friendship.

So much so, that he kept forgetting she was Amish and he was not.

He'd made such a big decision to leave the order, how could he ever even think about a woman who wasn't English?

What was going on with him? He wished he understood the reason he'd not looked at women for almost two decades, and now found himself thinking about the pair of them all the time.

Had God made his return to Jacob's Crossing so easy because he had another, far harder decision in store for him?

He was scrubbing a nonexistent spot on his counter, contemplating God and His will, when one of the old-timers called out as he was leaving. "See you, John. Have a good day."

"You, too, Jack," he replied. "Come back soon."

He would have said more, but the next words stuck in his throat. Because with Jack's exit, Mary and Abel entered.

He made an effort to greet them casually. "Hi, Mary . . . Abel. What can I get you?"

Abel trotted up to the case. "Hi, Mr. Weaver. I'm starving." Glancing back over his shoulder, he looked to his mom, who was his height. "Mamm, how many donuts can I have?"

Grinning, John leaned back against the wall behind the counter and crossed his arms over his chest.

Mary shook her head in wonder before she met John's gaze with a look of resigned amusement. "My son seems to have a bottomless pit for a stomach. Have you ever heard of such a thing?"

With a wink in Abel's direction, John nodded. "I was a boy once, Mary. My *mamm* often said the same thing about my brother Jacob and me."

"Oh! I didn't know you had a brother."

"Mamm, how many?" Abel interrupted.

"Oh, *boo*. I don't know. Three, perhaps?" Mary said and looked at John as if she was afraid he knew something about do-nut consumption that she didn't.

"Abel, there's a special going on today for twelve-year-olds. Four donuts for the price of three. Pick out four."

The boy grinned and started pointing.

Mary nibbled her bottom lip and watched, obviously worried that she was taking advantage of John.

She needn't have worried. He'd give the growing boy all the treats he wanted—if it meant they'd come in more often.

When Abel had chosen all four, John put them in a white paper sack and passed it right on to the boy. After a word of thanks, Abel took his sack and sat down near a pair of Amish men that he obviously knew.

Since they were almost alone, John let himself look at Mary more carefully. Today her dress was a dark teal. The color made her pretty skin look rosy and the brown of her hair look even richer. "Now, what can I get you, Mary?"

She looked at the case. Nibbled her lip some more. Then finally lifted her pale green–colored eyes to him. "A cinnamon roll?"

"You got it." He set it on a plate for her, then poured her a cup of coffee, leaving room for cream. Just the way she liked it.

When she handed him her money, he finally answered her question about his brother. "My brother was Jacob Weaver. He passed onto heaven almost three years ago. Do you remember him?"

"Oh. Oh, yes." Her expression turned sympathetic. "I'm sorry. I sometimes forget that you grew up Amish. I don't know why."

"It's fine." Actually, he kind of liked sharing bits about himself, little by little— instead of her already knowing about his family. It made him think they were on more even ground, since he knew next to nothing about her. "So, why isn't Abel in school today?"

"The teacher is taking the day off. Her child has the chicken pox."

"So you've had to rearrange your plans for the day?"

She smiled. "I don't mind. Abel is so busy—what with his school and his job, he hardly wants to spend time with me. This unexpected day off made me happy."

There was something so wistful about her expression, John couldn't help but feel for her. "Mary, may I have a cup of coffee with you?" he asked formally.

Just like he was at a tea party or something. *Sheesh!* The guys back at his old job would be having a field day with him.

Mary looked in Abel's direction. He was looking at a car magazine with the men. "That would be nice. I, um, will just sit here at the counter, if that's all right."

"It's perfect."

John poured himself a cup of coffee and then walked around the counter, taking a stool right next to her. They were close enough that her teal skirt brushed against his jeans.

Close enough to notice that she smelled fresh and clean, and faintly like lavender.

After she'd taken two bites of the treat, he said, "Mary, do you have a lot of help at home? It's just you and Abel, right?"

"Yes, it's just me and him. And I do have help. One of my neighbors helps with the yard once a month. And I support myself by sewing suits for the men in the community."

He knew how much effort went into a well-made suit. "That's hard work, Mary."

"It is," she agreed, flexing her fingers a bit as though they cramped up often. "But I only sew suits to help my funds—for extras. My William left me money."

The way she spoke of her husband gave him pause.

Made him wonder if she still grieved for him.

Since she'd brought it up, John gave in to his curiosity. "He passed away years ago, didn't he?"

"Eight years. Abel was only three. And I was only twenty-one."

John did a little mental math. Realized she was likely thirty, about eight years younger. "How did he die?"

"He had a brain aneurysm. It was a sudden thing." A shadow passed over her features, letting him know that the memory was still painful.

John felt his insides clench. He felt for her. "That had to be very hard."

"Oh, it was." She shook her head after a pause. "But until then, we had a *gut* marriage. My William was a good man. Kind and hardworking. We were lucky," she said softly.

"Yes, you were." She looked like she had been well loved and had a successful marriage. A little part of him was envious about that. At least she had good memories to keep.

All of his memories with Angela were tainted by his inability to be a good enough husband to her—and his inability to prove to her that he was ever going to shed all of his antiquated Amish ideals.

Struggling to not betray his emotions, John attempted to keep the conversation on things less personal. "You are lucky he had money in the bank," he said.

Of course, as soon as he uttered the words, he berated himself. Way to go, John. Nothing like focusing on money to make a woman feel like she was worthwhile.

But instead of looking offended, Mary nodded. "I've thought that a time or two. Actually, I'm grateful William was such a careful man with our finances. He

was like that—careful about most everything."

"That is fortunate." He shifted uncom-
fortably. Why was he suddenly jealous of
a dead man?

Mary continued, a sweet, faraway expression in her eyes. "See, William had a
cousin who'd died suddenly, and had left
his wife and family with little. She and her
kinner have really struggled." After taking a
fortifying sip of her coffee, she added, "I
think William was always afraid of something happening to him. Of leaving me without funds."

"But it's hard, still, isn't it? Being on your
own, I mean."

"Yes. Abel needs a father, or at least
an influence that's not so motherly." She
frowned slightly as she glanced over at
Abel's way. The boy seemed to be studi-
ously ignoring her—obviously anxious to
stay in the company of the men.

"Don't you have family nearby?"

"*Nee.* My parents moved to warmer cli-
mates when I married. I was the youngest by far. William was happy here, and
I was happy with him. Then, when he

passed, I didn't want to take Abel away from his home and everything that was familiar . . ." Her hand clenched. "He was already hurting so much."

John looked at her hand, saw how the knuckles were turning white, the stress of holding it all together taking its toll. He itched to grasp her hand. To gently unfold her fingers and smooth their tension.

But of course that would be exactly the wrong thing to do.

She blinked. "John, you seem like you know what it's like, to be married and then not. Did you suffer a loss, too? Are you a widower?"

Though telling her the truth made him uncomfortable, John didn't dare hide his past. "I was married, and I have known loss—but not from her death." Feeling like his tongue had become thick, he stumbled over the words. "Angela, my wife, left me."

Her eyes widened.

"I'm divorced."

"Oh."

Yeah. *Oh.* Though he still remembered the pain of receiving the divorce papers, of staring at the documents and realizing that all of his promises and vows could be broken with just a few pages of legal jargon, he now knew it had been for the best.

And all of it had happened long enough ago for him to smile about it. "I know. It's a bit of a shock to hear. Especially for you."

"Why especially for me?" Her voice had a slight edge to it.

"Because divorce doesn't happen when you're Plain." Belatedly, he realized he'd sounded a bit condescending—like, of course, Mary would have no understanding of his pain, or of what it had been like to tell people that his wife left him.

Because he wasn't good enough.

"Sorry. I didn't mean that the way it sounded. I sometimes fool myself into thinking that I wasn't devastated when Angela left me. I guess I'm still harboring some pain. And maybe some bitterness, too."

She sipped her coffee again. But when she spoke, her voice was noticeably cooler. "I can't imagine how hard that must have been." She blinked. "Sometimes, we talk so well together, I almost forget that we're so different."

"Yes. We are very different," he agreed. Feeling strangely deflated.

Because, really, what else could he say? It didn't matter if he thought she was pretty, or that he ached to be a better person for her.

Neither of them were young innocents. Life had happened, and with it they'd had successes and failures—and they carried those burdens with them. Neither badges of honor or scars of shame.

She scooted back in her stool from the counter. Not much, just an inch or two. But it was enough to further separate them. And enough to raise a wall between them, making sure the separation was there. Keeping them apart, reminding them that they were very different.

Abel walked up to them. "Mamm? Can we go soon? You said I could go fishing this afternoon, as soon as I finished my chores."

"It's not even nine yet, Abel. You'll have time."

Restless, he fidgeted from one foot to the other. "Well, are you almost done?"

It was on the tip of John's tongue to tell the boy to settle down and give his mother some space.

But of course he couldn't. It wasn't his place.

Most likely it would never be his place.

Mary pushed the half-eaten treat away from her. "*Jah*, child. I am finished. *Danke*, John."

"You're welcome," he said, watching them leave.

"Got any more coffee, John?" one of the men called out.

"Yeah . . . sure," he replied. With effort, he blocked out any longing he had for Mary. She was as off limits to him as so many worldly things had been to him years ago.

Before he'd changed and chosen a different path for himself. He needed to remember that.

And not recall that he actually had done everything he could to get those worldly things he'd wanted. That when he wanted something badly enough, he was willing to do whatever it took.

Yep. He hoped he would forget that real soon.

Chapter 6

Loyal had been easy to talk to. And so friendly and kind, too, Ella mused as she entered the library.

Though at first she'd feared he was only talking to her out of guilt, before long, Ella knew they were having a true conversation. Just like they had more in common than a farm.

Two women looked up from comfortable chairs near the nonfiction section. Ella smiled at them before continuing on to Ms. Donovan's office.

And though she knew she should be thinking about her first day of work, only thoughts of Loyal seemed to occupy her mind.

What would happen the next time they met? she wondered as she circled around two patrons standing in front of the new releases. Maybe she and Loyal would start talking nonstop, as though there had never been any awkwardness between them.

Just imagining that made her smile. Now wouldn't *that* be something?

Still daydreaming—and just steps from Ms. Donovan's door—Dorothy stopped her with a hand on her arm. "What did Loyal Weaver want? I saw him walking with you."

Ella looked at her curiously. "He wanted nothing. We were merely talking."

Slowly, Dorothy removed her hand, but she still stood too close. "What would you two have to talk about?"

"Nothing of importance." Ella stepped away, needing some space. Because Dorothy looked so worried, she attempted to lighten the mood. "Dorothy, why in the world are you asking me all these questions? Why do you care so much about what I say to Loyal?"

"Oh, no reason."

"Truly?"

Dorothy looked away, as if she was embarrassed. "I guess I care because we're such good friends now."

Now? "Dorothy, we've always been good friends . . ."

"Yes, of course," she said quickly with a flash of a smile. "But about Loyal, please don't trust him too much. Don't forget his true personality."

"I'm not sure what you're referring to." Ella shook her head, a thread of foreboding running through her. She didn't want to hear this. Didn't want to hear anything bad about Loyal. More than that, she didn't want to think about why Dorothy now looked so eager to pass on gossip.

"Loyal only thinks about himself, Ella. You know that, right?"

"Of course I don't know any such thing."

"You should. Handsome men like him are all the same, you know," Dorothy added, her words becoming firmer. Louder.

When an elderly lady glared in their direction, Dorothy circled a hand around Ella's elbow and started whispering. "You need to start ignoring him, Ella. That or tell him to leave you alone."

"All we were doing was walking," Ella

retorted, feeling more uncomfortable by the second. No matter what, she certainly wasn't going to start telling Loyal to leave her be. She'd been alone her whole life—long enough to appreciate a man's conversation. And, well, this was Loyal Weaver. The man for whom she'd held a secret infatuation. For years.

"He shouldn't be saying a word to you. Doesn't he know he already caused you enough pain?"

Ella didn't know whether she was more perturbed about Dorothy watching her movements from the windows or for her attitude. Her friend had no worries about sharing her opinions, that was for sure! "You have everything wrong. He only walked over to see if I wanted some donuts." She paused. "And to ask some questions about the house."

A look of smug pleasure entered her eyes. "Ah, so that's why he was talking to you. He wanted to gloat."

Though she was sure Dorothy hadn't intended to sound so mean, Ella's feelings were still hurt.

Was that all Dorothy thought she was ever going to be? Only worth talking to if it was about a farm? "Loyal was only being neighborly."

Dorothy looked her over before pursing her lips. "Perhaps. Oh, well, it doesn't matter now anyway," she said lightly. "Before long, we'll be so busy doing activities together, people like Loyal won't even be able to chat with you." She shrugged. "Plus, it ain't like you're neighbors now. Now you're my neighbor."

Adjusting the glasses on the bridge of her nose, Ella fought the urge to run away from Dorothy.

Dorothy truly wasn't making any sense. To her ears, it sounded as if her friend thought Ella intended to change everything about herself. Not just her place of residence, but her dreams and goals, too.

"I need to go. I need to go tell Ms. Donovan I'm here," she said, hating that her voice sounded almost desperate. "I am anxious to get started."

All the lines of worry on Dorothy's brow faded. "I almost forgot. *Jah!* Indeed, you'd better go in now before she counts you late."

Ella was beyond frustrated as she turned

to the door. If she was late, it had been because Dorothy hadn't let her go.

To her back, Dorothy spoke. "Now, don't worry if you don't understand everything right away. I'll help you."

Ella didn't bother to answer. Instead, she rolled her shoulders, hoping they'd relax as she shrugged off her doubts about Dorothy—and her confusing feelings about Loyal.

What mattered the most was making a good first impression. She wanted this job. She'd wanted this job—and her independence—more than anything she'd ever wanted in her life.

"Ms. Donovan, I'm here," she said after knocking on the head librarian's door.

With a spin of her chair, Jayne Donovan turned from computer to the front of her desk and held out her hand. "Hello, Ella. I see you're right on time, too."

Pure relief made Ella smile.

The manager smiled right back. "Now, first things first. From now on, you call me Jayne. Agreed?"

"All right."

"Well, that was easy. I think we're going

to get along just great," she said, putting Ella even more ease. "Now have a seat and let's get acquainted."

Within minutes, Ella found out Jayne was a transplant from Kentucky. She'd gotten two degrees at the university in Lexington. She wasn't married, either.

Every so often, a word would slip out with a Kentucky twang that made her seem all the more approachable. "Now, I have your paperwork for you to fill out. And after that, I thought I'd give you your first job—reading to the preschoolers."

Happiness filled her heart. This was what she'd dreamed about when Dorothy had first told her about the job. Ella wanted to be around children. "I would enjoy that."

"I had hoped you would. The three- and four-year-olds are darling, though a little rambunctious at times. But that's to be expected, I think. You do enjoy children, don't you?"

"I love children." Feeling more sure of herself, she confided, "I'm looking forward to having my own family one day."

"Well, if you ever have the desire to be around a houseful of children, let me know.

My sister has five children, and I seem to be their only babysitter."

"Anytime," Ella said, knowing she meant it. She was anxious to jump into her new life. Anxious to be so busy that she wouldn't think about Loyal using her old kitchen. Cooking on her old stove . . .

Or the tiny bit of new wariness she felt around Dorothy. She'd known Dorothy for years . . . but now, as she was living next door, Ella was wondering if maybe she hadn't really known her at all.

The problem with being five years old, Katie Weaver decided, was that nobody listened to you. Not her three older brothers—they were always too busy with their own plans to hear about hers.

Not her father, he was up in heaven with the angels. And though she supposed he did listen to her when she said her prayers, his listening didn't really count, 'cause she couldn't hear what he said right back.

Most times her mother paid attention to what she said—when she wasn't busy canning and gardening and cleaning. Or helping ladies organize things. Or helping Lucy and Calvin get settled in their new home, her parents' first house, on the other side of the barn.

For a while, Katie had followed Uncle John around, and would talk with him. But he was gone now, too, working in his donut shop and sleeping above it.

And today, not even Lucy was listening to her—which was really too bad, because back before Lucy became Calvin's wife, Katie had thought they'd talk and listen to each other all the time.

As she stared at Lucy, who was writing letters on the other side of the worn kitchen table, Katie sighed.

Lucy looked up in that distracted way of hers, caught Katie's eye, and then looked at her directly.

Finally.

"Why are you frowning at me?" her sister-in-law asked. "And furthermore, what has you so upset?"

"Nothin'."

"Oh, it's something, all right. All morning, all you've been doing is scowling." She looked down at her dress and apron, like she was afraid it was stained or something. "Have I done something to upset you?"

Before Katie could comment, Calvin

joined them. Right before her eyes, he walked right past Katie and kissed Lucy's cheek. Then smiled and kissed her again, but this time on the lips. Right there at the table! *Yuck!*

Katie sighed.

"What is wrong, dear?" Lucy asked.

"It's certainly nothing you've done," Calvin murmured before straightening and glaring in Katie's direction.

"I didn't say nothing," Katie blurted.

"Nothing of importance," Calvin countered, his voice clipped. And impatient, too.

Katie was just about to defend herself when he turned away from her—again— and bent over Lucy. And kissed her *again.*

Their third kiss.

"Don't mind Katie none," he murmured to Lucy, his voice all soft and gentle like flower petals from a daisy. "My little sister has always been like this. She stews more often than a watched pot."

Turning to Katie, he stood straight and glared at her. "You'd best wipe off that scowl, sister. No one wants to be frowned at by you."

"Well, no one wants to look at you kissing," she snapped right back. "You know you shouldn't be kissing at the table. *Three times.*" She held up three fingers for good measure.

Lucy's cheeks pinked. And Calvin's eyes narrowed.

He crossed his arms over his chest. "Katie, you're embarrassing Lucy. And furthermore, I, for one, have had enough of this new, saucy attitude of yours."

Though she felt a bit embarrassed for making Lucy uncomfortable, she jutted her chin out. "I don't have any saucy attitude." And she didn't think she did, either. Even if she wasn't quite sure what his comment meant.

"It's obvious that you do," her brother retorted. "And once more, if you don't—"

With a hand on his arm, Lucy intervened. "Settle down, Calvin. I'll talk to her," she said quietly.

Talk to her. Katie felt tears of frustration lick her eyelashes. Oh, she knew what *that* would entail: Lucy would talk and Katie would listen. Oh, but she was so tired of being made to feel like she was in the way.

"It's time you went back out to the fields," Lucy continued. "Graham's already there. He's probably lookin' for you."

"Perhaps," Calvin allowed.

With a soft smile, Lucy patted his arm. "Then you'd best get on your way, *jah*? You said you had a lot planned to do today."

Still glaring at Katie, he nodded. "I do. Then later, I told Loyal that I'd go help him a bit with his broken-down barn . . ."

Lucy stood up. "So it's time for you to leave. Go now."

"You'll be all right?"

"Of course, Calvin," she said sweetly. As Katie watched, Calvin kissed and hugged Lucy again, and even pressed his hands to her stomach and whispered to her. Right then, Lucy's lips curved upward and her eyes got all dreamy. Then, to her dismay, he kissed her yet again.

Kisses—four *and* five!

As soon as the kitchen door closed, Katie breathed a sigh of relief. Though she remembered her mother's lecture about how newlyweds needed time together, Katie thought this was a bit much. After all, they'd been married three months. Surely they'd been together enough?

Lucy cleared her throat. "Now, my dear little sister, do you care to tell me now what is wrong?"

"Do you even want to listen?"

"Of course I do."

"Really?"

"Katie Weaver, you need to adopt a better tone of voice. Now. I don't want to hear you be so whiney."

Katie weighed her options. It was becoming obvious that she could either try once again to get someone to listen to her, or she was going to have to give up. But that would mean she'd be stuck sitting by herself in her room.

"Lucy, two weeks ago during supper I said I wanted to go to the library. Do you remember?"

She looked at Katie curiously. "I do."

"Every morning, I try to get someone to take me, but they're too busy."

"This is a busy house," Lucy murmured.

"Too busy for me. And I don't like that. I'm important, too."

Little by little, Lucy's lips curved upward. "Indeed you are," Lucy said softly. After a pause, she said, "Katie, why do you want to go to the library so badly? Do you really need a new book?"

"My girlfriend Mary said they have a

summer reading program there. She started on practically the first day off from school."

"Ah. Now I'm beginning to understand. You want to join it, too?"

"I do. Mary said she takes books home and reads them, and then when she goes back, she gets stickers on a chart. I bet I'm going to be the only student at school who won't be able to show the teacher a star chart."

"Which would be a difficult thing."

Katie quickly looked at Lucy just to see if she was laughing at her. But Lucy's gaze was sweet and kind. So she added, "I want to join. And I'm trying to be patient, but my patience is almost all gone."

"I can see that it is."

"I'm trying, but I don't have all that much patience, anyway." She shook her head sadly. "I don't know why."

"It's one of the Lord's mysteries, for sure."

"Anyway, no one will take me to the library and I'm too small to take myself."

After another long look her way, Lucy started straightening up her writing supplies and set them in a basket. "You know what? You are exactly right. It isn't fair that no one has taken the time to take you."

"I am?" She shook her head. "I mean, really?"

"Indeed. Two weeks is a mighty long time to be patient. And you have done a *gut* job."

"You think so?" She really did want someone to think she was a good girl.

Lucy chuckled. "Oh, Katie, you do make me laugh! I had forgotten all about my promise to take you to the library. I am sorry."

"Graham had promised, too, but he started thinking about Jenna."

"And Loyal has the new farm."

"And Mamm has the house and her chores. Calvin has you," Katie blurted, then immediately wished she hadn't. Calvin had told her many times that he wanted everyone to be nice to Lucy all the time. And that they should always make her happy and welcome.

Katie was pretty positive that he wasn't going to like her saying such things to Lucy.

But instead of frowning, a dimple appeared in Lucy's cheek. Katie almost sighed in relief. That dimple was a sure sign that she was amused, not angry or hurt.

"Let's put on our bonnets and hitch up the buggy and go, then."

"You mean we can go right now?"

Lucy tilted her head to one side. "Can you think of a better time?"

"No . . ."

"Then I think we'd best get going. After all, to tell you the truth, I'm a little afraid of what might happen if we make you be any more patient."

"My *mamm* says I have a lot to learn about waiting." Lowering her voice, Katie confided, "I'm not too good at waiting, either."

Lucy laughed again. "Let's go, Katie. And guess what? When we sign you up, we'll sign me up for the program, too."

"You're going to read a bunch of books?"

"Why not? I enjoy reading. And it will give you and me something of our own to do together." She clapped her hands. "So, today, we'll sign up and check out some books as well."

"Danke."

"It's no trouble, Katie," she said softly.

Stepping closer, Katie reached out for Lucy's hand. "I'm sorry if I made you sad."

"You didn't," she said, giving her hand a gentle squeeze. "I, for one, am glad your *bruder* Calvin married me. He makes me happy. But, you know what else?"

Katie shook her head no.

"You do, too," Lucy said with a smile.

Katie grinned right back. Maybe people listened after all.

Chapter 7

Ella loved working at the library. There was always plenty to do, she was surrounded by lots of people to talk with, and every day at noon she got to read a book to the children.

Picking out which book she would read aloud was the first activity she did each morning. She'd comb the children's section, looking for books that were bright and cheerful and amusing. Every read-aloud book should be like that, she thought. Those books needed to inspire small children to develop a love for literature and learning, too.

Precisely at noon, she picked up her book and walked to the area designated with a large braided rug and a comfortable wooden rocking chair. Twenty children were sitting there—some by themselves, some with their mothers or fathers.

"Oh, what a nice group we have today," she said when they all looked up expectantly. "I'm happy to see each one of you."

Almost as one, the small group of children scooted closer. Peering at her, they seemed to be weighing her attributes. Ella held herself still as they looked at her tall frame, her big feet, her glasses.

Though she'd long given up trying to look smaller than she was, this was one of the few instances where she certainly did wish she was as petite and lovely as Calvin's wife, Lucy.

Lucy never failed to look like an angel, and Ella had noticed more than one man look at Calvin's bride with admiration.

Ella didn't fault them. Still, she couldn't help but wonder what it would be like for someone like Loyal Weaver to think she was attractive.

Oh, for heaven's sakes! When was she

ever going to move on from Loyal? Years and years of waiting had shown that she was not ever going to be the woman for him. She needed to start looking for someone else. Surely there were other men in the world who she would take a fancy to.

With effort, she pushed all thoughts of him away and concentrated on the adorable faces in front of her.

As they peered at her, and she smiled right back, a few waved to her. Others scooted closer.

"What are you going to read today?" a boy in the front row asked.

"It's a funny book that is going to need your help, children." Holding up the bright cover, she grinned as many of the boys and girls stared in wonder at it. "It's called *Chicka Chicka Boom Boom.*"

To her pleasure, the whole group started to giggle.

"The title made me giggle, too," she said. "Do you think all of you could say it?"

One by one, each child called out the book's title. Earning lots of laughter—and scowls from a pair of elderly men reading the paper in the back corner.

Ella didn't let their displeasure worry her too much, though. Signs clearly announced that there was a children's story time three days a week at noon. If a person really was looking for peace and quiet, he should take care to sit far from the reading area.

And anyway, Ella figured a twenty-minute story, filled with laughter and the merry sound of children's voices, had to make even the most hardened of irritable people lighter of heart.

"Let's begin," she said, folding the title page back of the bold purple-and-green-colored book. "*Chicka Chicka Boom Boom* by Mr. Bill Martin, Jr. and Mr. John Archambault." She looked around. Most of the children were sitting cross-legged, fidgeting. And some of their parents were looking at her warily. As if they'd hoped for something far different than a story involving such nonsensical words.

Ella's nerves sang. This was only her third time to read aloud. The other two times had been successes, but perhaps each time wasn't going to be as easy as she'd hoped.

Well, there was only one thing to do, and that was to try her best. After clearing her throat, she opened up to the first page, smiled at the wonderful bright, blocky drawings, and began: "'A told B, and B told C, "I'll meet you at the top of the coconut tree.'"

One by one, all the eyes of the *kinner* lit up and smiles of pure joy lit their faces. Ella found herself smiling, too. Oh, but she loved these storybooks!

Page by page, she read the silly alphabet story, delighting in the children's enthusiasm.

Especially one little girl's enthusiasm. By the time Ella was reading about "Q,R,S, and T," she'd realized who that girl was— Katie Weaver. It had been some time since she'd seen the child, and even longer since she'd tried to put a name to her. Over the last two years, Ella's attendance at church had been sketchy at best. And the days when she had gone, she'd been so worried about her mother, she'd hardly done more than quickly nod a greeting to everyone before escorting her home.

But now, as she closed the book, Ella couldn't help but notice that Katie had scooted so close, she was almost at her feet.

"*Kinner,* thank you for coming today. That is the end of that."

Broad grins and spontaneous clapping greeted her words.

"That was a *gut buch*, Miss Hostetler," one of the parents said as she walked forward to claim her child. "You chose well."

"*Danke.* It is one of my favorites."

The woman's son spontaneously hugged her knees, and Ella smiled and patted his shoulder. "I'm glad you had fun today. Maybe I'll see some of you another time?"

"You will. Thank you, Miss Ella," he said.

A few others chorused the same sentiments as they left.

Ella waved goodbye to them. Then couldn't help but notice Katie Weaver was standing at her side, patiently waiting.

"Hello, Katie. How may I help you?"

After a glance toward Lucy, who she'd just realized was sitting on a chair by one of the windows knitting, Katie puffed up her chest a bit. "I want to do the summer reading program."

Katie sounded so very solemn, and her posture was so stiff and assured, Ella crossed her arms over her chest, mimicking the girl's stance. "Is that so?" she teased.

"Uh-huh. Is it too late?"

Belatedly, Ella realized that this was a very important topic for the girl. "Not at all," she said softly. "Come with me, and I'll give you the information." Ella looked beyond Katie's head and smiled at Calvin Weaver's new wife. "Hello, Lucy. We've met before, but you might not remember. I'm Ella."

"Of course I remember meeting you." She stepped forward, all golden eyes and hair. "It's nice to see you. You are a *gut* storyteller."

The praise made her feel wonderful. But as she eyed Lucy's delicate beauty, she started to feel awkward once again.

But almost as quickly, she shrugged off that feeling of insecurity. Lucy couldn't help her looks any more than Ella could. And obviously, they were of no concern to Ella. "So, Lucy, how are you enjoying Jacob's Crossing?"

"I am enjoying it very much," she replied with a friendly smile. "Especially this morning's visit to the library. I liked that *Chicka Chicka Boom Boom* book."

"I do as well. I think I enjoy the books as

much as the *kinner*," she confided as she led the way to the circulation desk and a pile of brochures about the reading program.

Leaning down a bit, she showed the girl the packet. "Katie, every time you read a book, we're going to give you a stamp," she said, flipping the first page back. "At the end of the summer, we'll give you stamps and perhaps even a special prize."

"I want to read lots of books." She looked toward Lucy. "She does, too."

Lucy set a novel on the counter. "May I have a reading chart too, Ella?"

"Well, of course." After giving Lucy a packet and stamping Lucy's book, Ella started to turn away. But Katie stopped her with a little tug of her sleeve. "Miss Ella, do you work every day?"

"Almost. I work four days of the six a week. The library is always closed on Sundays."

"I'm going to come back to see you."

"I hope so." Turning toward Lucy, she smiled again. "I hope you both do."

After they said their goodbyes, Ella went back and rearranged some of the pillows and things that had gotten thrown about when the children had come.

Ms. Donovan joined her. "Ella, I want to let you know that we are so happy you're here. Already, we've noticed an increase in children during story time. Two mothers who had never been to the library before confided to me that they specifically came because they heard you were such a wonderful storyteller."

"That makes me happy to hear."

"I'm glad." Patting her forearm, Jayne smiled broadly. "You're a terrific addition to our staff."

"*Danke.* I mean, thank you," Ella said with a smile. "I'm glad to be here, for sure."

"I think it's your lunchtime now."

"Yes. I'll eat my sandwich then work at the circulation desk."

"Take your full thirty minutes, Ella. We don't want to wear you out."

"I'll be fine." Oh, if Jayne only knew how easy were her days compared to those of her previous life. Living isolated on the farm, keeping up with the garden, laundry, and cooking—added to the necessary time spent caring for her mother—her days had been exhausting.

Here things were a little scary but mighty fulfilling, too.

The rest of the hours flew by and before she knew it, she was walking home by Dorothy's side. She seemed especially withdrawn and quiet, barely offering much more than one-word answers to Ella's comments.

Only later did Ella remember that not once did Dorothy say a word about her success and Jayne Donovan's praise.

No, if anything, her friend and neighbor only looked angry about it.

Later that evening, Ella invited Dorothy over for cobbler. Dorothy had done a lot for her, and Ella wanted to make sure she didn't feel taken advantage of.

When she'd first arrived, Dorothy still seemed sullen. But by the time she ate her last bite, she seemed more like her usual self. "I don't know how you managed to make a peach cobbler today," she said, finally thawing a bit. "But I'm glad you did. It was tasty."

"*Danke.* It was my mother's favorite recipe. And it's very easy to make, you know. All you really need are the right products on hand to put it together in a snap."

"Where did you find the peaches?"

"Corrine brought them by today."

Dorothy stilled. "I didn't notice her buggy."

"She walked here from her home."

"That far?"

"It's only a forty-minute walk." Feeling awkward, Ella added, "Corrine enjoys the exercise. Plus she knows how much I like to see her."

"She seems to go out of her way for you."

"She does," Ella said with a smile. "She's always been a *gut* friend."

"But doesn't she have a husband and family?"

Ella hesitated for a moment. "Of course. Dorothy, what is wrong? You're acting like you don't understand why Corrine would come visit me."

"I'm merely surprised you two are such *gut* friends. Still."

Dorothy's conversation was definitely taking some getting used to, Ella reflected. She was so blunt and seemed to have no problem saying what was on her mind, at any time. "Why would you be surprised? Corrine is a very nice woman."

"You have nothing in common."

"We do. We've been friends for years, since we were small. Corrine and I used to trade sandwiches at lunchtime. I never liked my mother's ham sandwiches." She grinned, remembering the memories. "Of course, I never told my *mamm,* so she continued to pack me ham sandwiches."

But Dorothy wasn't even smiling. In fact, she looked confused.

With some surprise, Ella realized that because Dorothy was ten years older than herself, she'd never gone to school with her.

And so she'd never seen just what good friends she and Corrine really were.

Attempting to fill Dorothy in, Ella kept talking. "When I first started school, I didn't have my glasses. Living on the farm the way we did, neither of my parents had much time to teach me my letters. When I went to school, it was the first time I had to see a chalkboard. Or try to read the tablets in front of me." Smiling faintly at the memory, Ella shook her head. "Well, I couldn't see anything. It all looked like fuzzy worms. But I was too shy to tell the teacher, so everyone thought I was dumb."

"That's horrible!"

Remembering the pain of those days,

Ella nodded. "It was difficult. But Corrine sat right next to me at lunch and offered to help me. As a matter of fact, she was the one who realized I had a vision problem, not a reading problem."

"What did your parents say?"

"They were terribly relieved. Glasses were easy to get, and they made my life much better. Obviously, I have a lot to be grateful to her for." Well, until everyone stopped calling her "Dumb Ella" and switched to "Four-eyed Ella." Of course, later, they called her "Plain Ella," but she wasn't eager to share all this.

"Now, though, you and Corrine probably don't have much to talk about."

"Oh, we still do. Corrine and I have a friendship so deep that even if we couldn't see each other for a month, it would seem like we hadn't been apart for five minutes."

"Still, being a wife and mother is far different than living on your own and being a librarian."

"Perhaps, but situations change, don't you think?"

"Corrine's won't change all that much. Even when her kids are grown, you won't have those experiences. And then she'll be looking forward to weddings and grand-children. You'll have none of that."

Stung, Ella stood up and carried their dessert bowls to the sink and started rinsing them off. "Dorothy, when I said that a situation would change, I was talking about my situation."

"You think?"

"Well, *jah.* One day I'll be married. One day I'll have *kinner* and will be taking them to the library to be read to instead of being the one reading." Even thinking about that made Ella smile. She could hardly wait to find the right man and begin living even more of her dreams.

One of Dorothy's thick eyebrows rose. "You truly think that will happen to you?"

Ella tried not to let her feelings get hurt. Dorothy was just blunt, not cruel. "Well, I hope and pray that's the case. I want to be a wife and mother." Quietly, she added, "Every morning, I say my devotions and visit with God. I give him my thanks. And tell him that I'm so happy with his blessings, and am looking forward to finding out what else he has in store for me."

A pinched look crossed Dorothy's expression, one filled with doubt and scorn. Ella was shaken up by its intensity.

Where had that come from? Had Dorothy always harbored feelings so bitter and dark that Ella had been blind to?

Her words more fierce than ever, she said, "And do you really think He listens to you? To Ella Hostetler?"

"Of course," Ella said, shocked that Dorothy would even ask such a thing. "The Lord always listens. He's part of my world."

"Just like me?"

"No, not just like you," Ella said quietly. "He guides my life and makes everything clearer."

"I doubt that."

"I'm sorry to hear you say that," Ella said, completely sincere. "I love being one with the Lord. I had hoped you felt the same way."

But instead of nodding in agreement, Dorothy looked even more confused and disgruntled. Standing up abruptly, she said, "I need to leave."

"All right. Are you working tomorrow?"

"I am," Dorothy said, but didn't offer to walk with Ella.

Going with Dorothy to the door, Ella opened it, saying, "Thank you for coming over."

Dorothy merely walked out, leaving Ella feeling chilled.

Even in the hot August air.

Chapter 8

Over a week had passed since he'd last seen Mary. John Weaver took that as a sign that it was time to stop thinking about things he couldn't have—and to focus on things he could.

Like maybe a date with Jayne Donovan.

Of course, asking her out was proving to be just as awkward as anything he'd ever done. From the moment she picked up the phone, he was stumbling over himself, trying to come up with the right words.

"So, I was hoping, if you weren't doing anything Saturday night, you might like to have dinner with me," John finished, clutching his phone a little tighter. Closing his eyes as his words echoed in his ear.

For heaven's sakes! He sounded like an idiot! No, like a child. Like a pimply-faced teenager trying to find the courage to ask his first girl out for ice cream.

Not like a thirty-eight-year-ago grown man who was asking the town librarian out to dinner. The librarian! It wasn't like she was a movie star or anything.

No, she was just beautiful and funny, and he thought about her way too much in the middle of the night.

The pause lengthened on the other end of the line. Obviously she was trying to find a way to let him down easily.

John bit his lip so he wouldn't do something stupid, like beg.

"John?"

"Yes?"

"I . . . I hate to admit this, but . . ."

While she paused he wondered if he could live the rest of his life in Jacob's Crossing and never see her again. The humiliation was too much.

"I've promised a girlfriend that I would dog-sit her dachshund."

He wasn't following her. He was getting rejected because of a wiener dog? "Oh."

She chuckled. "What I'm trying to say—not very well—is, on Saturday I work from nine until three, and Minnie gets lonely."

"Minnie, the dachshund?"

"Yes. Boy, I guess you can tell I'm nervous, huh? What I'm trying to say, is . . . would you mind coming over and I'll make you dinner?"

His mouth went dry. She wasn't rejecting him. Instead, she wanted to cook for him. All because she was the kind of person who took care of wiener dogs for friends.

"Jayne, I wouldn't mind that at all." Oh, he hoped he didn't sound too awkward.

"Are you sure? I know it's not a dinner out . . ."

"I live alone. I'd love a home-cooked meal," he said in a rush. "That is, if it's not too much trouble, what with the wiener dog and everything."

"It's not at all. Do you like steaks?"

He was now the luckiest man in the world. "I love steak."

"Oh, good. I thought maybe we could

grill, and I'll just throw together a salad and pop some potatoes in the oven."

Eager to help in some way, he asked, "How about I pick up a pie from the bakery?"

"I would absolutely love that. If you pick up anything chocolate, you'll be my favorite person in the world."

"I'll do my best," he promised, smiling alone in his living room. After he hung up the phone, John knew he would go to at least a dozen restaurants and bakeries if it meant he could bring her a chocolate pie.

After all, it had been a very long time since he had been any woman's favorite person.

As Loyal handed Graham yet another piece of yellowed linoleum, he blew at the hair that seemed determined to stick to his brow. "Next time I buy a house in the middle of August, remind me not to pull up the linoleum and carpet right away."

Graham grunted as he tossed the scrap into the trash pile and held out his hands for more. "I'll tell you one thing, I'm definitely going to be sure I never volunteer to help you again. This is a *schlimm* job."

As he felt yet another line of sweat drip down his back, Loyal couldn't help but agree. "It *is* an awful job. But even you have to admit that it's necessary. These coverings need to go. Underneath is lovely wood. It's a shame it's been covered up for so long."

"Perhaps," Graham allowed as he grabbed another piece and tossed.

"Perhaps? This plastic floor is yellowed and curling. Wood flooring will be much better underfoot."

"Who are you getting to help you sand and stain and varnish? 'Cause it's surely not going to be me."

Loyal had counted on that. He'd wanted to make sure he spent his money in a smart way. Instead of trying to refurbish the floors himself, he'd decided to hire professionals. "I'm hiring the Johnson Brothers from Middlefield. They said work was slow, so they can begin tomorrow. They're going to let me help, too, so the labor costs won't be too high."

Graham raised his brows. "At least they'll get paid. All I'm getting is sweaty."

"A little hard work never hurt anyone."

"And now you sound like Calvin."

That caught Loyal off guard. Their brother was notoriously opinionated and bossy. But now that he was a home and a landowner himself, Loyal started thinking that maybe being bossy wasn't a bad idea. With ownership came responsibilities.

"Well, at least we're all done now," Loyal said as he got to his feet. "After I sweep everything up, it will be ready for the Johnsons to begin."

"I'll start carrying this linoleum to the wagon. But I have to warn you, I'm leaving you at six o'clock this evening, whether you are ready for me or not."

"What are you doing that is so important?"

"I'm taking Jenna Yoder out for a drive tonight," Graham said with a somewhat secretive smile.

"I had no idea you two were seeing each other. When did that come about?"

"Only recently. I stopped by to see Jenna the other day and we got to talking. Then we agreed to go on this drive. She's *schee*, don't you think?"

Loyal couldn't help but think that his brother was being more than a little blasé about it all. And if he knew his brother—

which he did—Loyal knew that Graham never did much without carefully weighing the pros and cons. "Yes, Jenna is very pretty. But I thought you had a special relationship with Mattie Lapp. What happened there?"

"Nothing." He sputtered. "Actually, I'm fairly surprised you asked that. Mattie and I are just friends, you know. There's nothing special between us."

Loyal thought the complete opposite. Whenever Graham and Mattie were in the same room, sparks flew.

But he surely wasn't going to let Graham know that if he wasn't ready to hear it. "I guess I didn't realize you two were only friends. I thought the two of you would court one day."

"To be honest, one day I thought we might as well," Graham said after a lengthy pause. "But Mattie has made it plain time and again that I'm only her friend and that's all she ever wants me to be. It's time to move on."

Despite wanting to push his brother on this decision, Loyal had learned from watching Calvin that it wasn't possible to control one's heart—or one's future. The Lord liked to have a say in just about everything. And sometimes, it was best if you just let Him have his way. He had to trust God would turn things around if He wanted.

"I hope you and Jenna have a good time," he said simply. "I wish you both well."

Graham nodded his thanks, then paused as he was picking up the linoleum. "What about you?"

"What do you mean?"

"Aren't you interested in any woman yet?"

A sudden vision of Ella Hostetler appeared in his mind, but he shook it away. "*Nee*. But it's just as well, you know. I've got a lot to do."

"We all are busy. But finding someone special is a good thing."

"Perhaps."

"And you know all the girls have always been by your side. More than one has said you're the best looking of us three."

"Looks mean nothing."

"To some it does."

"If you have to leave me to go courting, we had better get to work," Loyal said, suddenly eager to push the conversation away from him.

"I'm working. I'm working. And sweating," Graham grumbled as he picked up his load and walked outside again.

As Loyal moved to the edge of the carpet and pulled, he thought of Ella once again. And wondered if she'd ever wanted to pull up all of this carpet and enjoy wood floor underneath.

He wondered how her day had been at the library.

And he thought about her smile when he dopily talked about donuts.

More times during the day than he could count, he'd found himself thinking about Ella. And that made him a bit uncomfortable. How could he have known someone all his life, but suddenly start seeing her in a new way?

It didn't make sense. With relief, he saw their uncle's truck approach. "Uncle John's here. He said he'd bring in supplies from town. Come help me unload, wouldja?"

"Sure," Graham said, already striding forward to visit with John.

Chapter 9

"Mattie, I'm so glad you are feeling *gut* again," Lucy said as they walked along the well-worn path between their two homes. "Now we can walk together as often as we'd like."

"As often as I'd like, maybe," Mattie corrected. "I have a feeling if you had your way, we'd walk together every single day."

"Maybe. It is such a pleasure to be outside. And to have free time."

Mattie looked at her friend fondly. If she was making big improvements on the inside, it was Lucy, surely, who had made the biggest difference on the outside.

To compare her appearance to the way she was last year was to compare night and day. Calvin Weaver's love had changed so much. Where she used to be timid and unsure, now Lucy was more confident.

Her cheeks were flushed and pink, her eyes were brighter, even her posture was different. While Lucy had always been a beauty, now she was certainly glowing.

"It is such a blessing that you found love with Calvin. Now that you live so close, it's almost like we're sisters."

"I can't believe our good fortune," Lucy agreed. "I do love living near you."

"And you love Calvin, still?"

"Oh, yes!" When Mattie started laughing, Lucy's cheeks turned bright pink. "I mean, Calvin is certainly a blessing to me."

Though she ached to tease Lucy some more, Mattie didn't. Lucy was finally so happy, there was no way Mattie was ever going to do a thing to disrupt that happiness. "I'm sure he is a blessing."

Lucy looked her way, and then laughed again. "I know I sound just like a teenager after her first date. But I can't help it, you see. Calvin is so different than Paul."

"I would hope so!"

"No, I mean, he is always sweet and gentle. And so patient, too." Her eyes clouded. "Some nights I still have bad dreams about my life with Paul. I wake up with my pulse racing and my body sweating." She shook her head in wonder. "Yet Calvin never complains. He just holds me close."

A momentary twinge of jealousy rose up, strong and fierce. With all her will, Mattie pushed it aside. It didn't matter that she didn't have someone like that in her life.

And it was just as well, too. The last thing she needed was to have someone to love who she would surely lose when the cancer came back.

No, it was simply better to get used to living on her own. And being grateful for her blessings. She'd survived cancer. That should be enough for anyone.

To ask to be happy too, well, that would be too much to ask.

John Weaver soon found out that locating a chocolate pie in Middlefield hadn't been all that difficult. He'd ended up asking Amos where to go. And though the man was as crusty as a piece of day-old bread, he knew his food.

"Go to Holtzman's," he said without hesitation. "They make a silk chocolate pie that will make a person's toes curl, it's so good."

Well, that reaction sounded a little extreme, but John figured he'd give it a try. After all, Jayne had seemed like she put a lot of emphasis on that particular dessert.

At five minutes after seven, he rang her doorbell. Immediately, he heard the frantic barking of a tiny dachshund.

Jayne opened the door with a harried smile. "John. You're here!"

He held up his box. "I brought pie."

Her eyes lit up. "I can't tell you how happy that makes me. I wanted to have everything perfect for you, but I left work late. Now we know dessert, at least, will be good."

Those words were enough to set his pulse beating a little quicker. Right that minute, John could care less about steaks. All he needed was Jayne to keep saying things like that.

With effort, he forced himself to act cool

and collected. "I don't need perfect. How can I help?"

With a grateful smile, she handed him a lighter. "Could you go to my porch and start the grill? I'm just finishing up the salad."

"Sure." After following her to her kitchen, stepping over a barking Minnie the whole time, John placed his box on the counter, took the lighter, and went out to her grill. To his dismay, the little dog followed at his heels, barking and baring her teeth, circling him like a shark.

"Dog, don't you do something foolish," he warned as he stepped over it, turned on the gas, and lit the grill. "I can't say I'd be all that understanding if you bit my ankle."

"John, have a seat. I'll be right out," Jayne said through the screened window.

"All right," he called back, trying not to notice that the dog's barks were becoming fiercer.

With one more glare at the little red-haired wiener dog, he walked right past it and took a seat at the black wrought-iron dining set.

Minutes later, Jayne came out with a tray

of iced tea. The minute she appeared, Minnie lay down next to them and fell silent.

Glad for the reprieve, John stood up to help Jayne, taking the tray from her in an easy movement. In the handoff, his fingers brushed hers.

Jayne stilled, looked at him in wide-eyed wonder for a moment.

John swallowed and tried to think of something sweet to say that didn't sound too forward.

As the dog bit his ankle.

"Ach!" he said with a jerk, toppling the plastic glasses on the tray. "Jayne, hey, I'm sorry—" he began as the dog growled and circled again.

He jerked away, sending the glasses to the ground. Tea sprayed out. The little dog whimpered and ran away.

"Oh!" Jayne said again, grabbing the tray from him and plopping it on the table. "Oh, John. That dog!" She bit her lip. "I don't know what could be wrong with her. She's usually such a sweetie . . ."

He glared at the dachshund's retreating back end. "Except when she's biting people."

She pulled him to a chair. "I'm so sorry. Are you okay?"

"I'm fine. She didn't break the skin," he said. "Well, hardly," he corrected, seeing the tiny bite mark. Well, that's what he got for wearing flip-flops with his jeans. If he'd had on boots, no damage would have been done.

Jayne bit her lip again, her eyes tearing up.

Now he felt terrible. It wasn't like it was her fault the little wiener dog was a menace!

Without thinking, he reached for her hand. "Jayne? I'm sorry. Did I break all your glasses?"

"It's not that. They're plastic. Oh, John. I'm so sorry."

Linking his fingers through hers, he eyed her again, then couldn't help but chuckle. "Jayne, I spilled the tea all over your shirt."

She looked down at her floral blouse in dismay. Then, to his surprise and pleasure, she started giggling. "I look horrible. And Minnie bit you. What a terrible first date."

"I wouldn't have it any other way," he

said. "I was nervous and now, well, I think it's all uphill from here."

Her eyes widened. "You were nervous, too?"

"Jayne, it took me two weeks to ask you to dinner."

"I didn't think you were *ever* going to ask!"

Slowly, he pulled back his hand. He could have held it all night, but John thought it was probably best to let her put on a fresh shirt. "How about you change and I'll put the steaks on?"

"That sounds perfect," she said with a sigh. "Thanks. I'll be right back. And I'll lock up Minnie in my room."

"I think that sounds like a fantastic idea."

He smiled at her as she walked away. For the life of him, he couldn't ever recall having a better laugh with a woman.

The rest of the evening passed in a blur of easy conversation and flirty glances. They talked about their pasts, and about their futures, and even about little Katie Weaver.

The pie was as good as Amos had proclaimed.

When it came time for him to leave, John kissed her on the cheek, though he instinctively knew that if he'd moved his lips to the left just a few inches, she would have welcomed them just fine.

Just after 10:30, he reversed his truck down her driveway and realized that, if he didn't put the car windows down, he would be able to continue inhaling the faint scent of gardenias lingering on his clothes.

He was still thinking about those eyes of hers, and the way they'd sparkled in amusement while sharing a story about Katie bossing him around, when he happened to see an Amish woman walking on the sidewalk beside a tall, lanky teenaged boy. The boy had a youthful swagger in his stride—obviously he didn't care to be seen walking by his mother's side.

The mother's hands were primly clasped in front of her. Her posture was erect, her chin up. But her expression was so sad, John did a double take through his rear-view mirror.

Then he felt a lump in his throat.

The woman was Mary. For a second, he thought about pulling over. Seeing if they wanted a ride. But of course that would have been too pushy. He hardly knew them, and it was obvious Mary was in no mood for conversation.

John found himself worrying about Mary and her boy all night.

Chapter 10

Ella's favorite time of the day was the morning. It had always been that way. Each morning, she'd wake with the sunrise and start a pot of coffee brewing. Then she'd take out whatever devotional she was reading and spend her first half hour with the Lord.

She'd sit in her rocking chair, the one her grandfather had built for her mother, and rock while reading and praying. As the sky grew brighter, her whole being would fill with joy and happiness.

Only then would she sip her first cup of coffee and get dressed.

On the farm, she'd have a great many things to do after that. She'd tend to the animals and the garden, clean up the kitchen. And attend to her mother, of course.

But now Ella had only her one plate and one cup to wash after her breakfast of toast and fruit. It took no time to make her bed and set her little home to rights. And since she didn't start work until nine in the morning, she had time on her hands.

When she'd sat on the bench with Corrine during the auction, just imagining such emptiness brought her to tears. But, actually, the opposite was becoming true. Having extra time was an unexpected pleasure.

For the first time in her twenty-two years, she was enjoying the gift of rest and relaxation. So much so, that some days her mind spun with ideas for all the possibilities.

In the winter, she planned to sew and quilt. But now, in the middle of summer, she couldn't resist tending to the three pots of flowers she'd set on the edge of her small back porch. And, of course, reading one of the many books she checked out at the library.

At the moment, she was knee deep in a series by Karen Kingsbury. She'd just finished a chapter and looked at her kitchen clock, mentally weighing the pros and cons of reading a second chapter, when there was a knock at her door.

Stifling a groan, she went to answer it. Dorothy had taken to checking up on her day and night. Ella knew she was going to have to find a way to gently tell her that she was used to being alone a bit more.

Perhaps today was the day to do that.

As she twisted the knob, she mentally prepared herself to give Dorothy the news.

"Hi," Loyal Weaver said.

"Loyal? What are you doing here?"

Flashing a grin, he said the obvious. "Visiting you?"

Still trying to wrap her brain around his appearance, she looked him up and down. "Is anything the matter?"

"No." He shifted. "May I come in? I was over at the donut shop, but I didn't see you walk by this morning."

"No. I don't have to be at work until nine-thirty today." She stepped backward to allow him access.

Loyal didn't even hesitate.

After she closed the door, she leaned back against it, staring at him. Staring at him right there in her house. Here, in her living room, Ella felt dwarfed by his presence. He really was tall, and so terribly handsome. And the way he looked at her—just like there was more to her than she'd ever thought—it made her heart beat a little bit faster.

He took off his straw hat and shook his hair. She couldn't look away, his blond hair was so striking against his tan skin.

"I have some coffee, if you'd like?"

"No. Listen, I was wondering if you'd like to come out to the farm this evening. When you're done with work."

She was stunned. "Why?"

"Well, I thought you might want to see your horse. And, I thought you might like to see what I've been doing to your house. I pulled out the old linoleum and carpet. And today, some workers came and sanded and stained. It looks nice."

She noticed he kept referring to the things as hers—obviously he was trying hard to not overstep. "I bet it does. I . . . I always would have preferred to feel smooth wood planks under my feet, but we could never afford to do that project."

"So will you come over?"

His enthusiasm was contagious and disconcerting! The last thing in the world she wanted to do was once again become emotionally involved with her property again.

To do so would be to take a giant step backward, and that wasn't what she was about. She was now stepping forward and looking toward her future.

"Loyal, it's no longer *my* house," she pointed out, trying to sound upbeat—or at least all right with the idea. "The farm and the house are *yours*."

"It's only been mine for a few days."

"But it still is yours. And, while you're very kind to offer to let me see it, you mustn't feel guilty."

"I don't," he said quickly, his blue eyes flashing.

"No?"

As his eyes skimmed her face, he shook his head in frustration. "I'm handling this all wrong, aren't I?"

"There is no one way—"

"Listen, I'm not offering the invitation out of guilt."

What other reason could there be? "Then why?"

"I'm offering because I know you loved the place, too. I . . . I mean, I thought you did."

"I did," she said quickly. Speaking the truth. "I lived there my whole life, of course."

"Then I'm sure you have some feelings about improvements you'd like to see. Don't you? These are big changes I'm proposing, but exciting ones. I simply want someone else to share that with me. What's wrong with that?"

"Nothing, of course." But even as she answered, Ella knew she was fooling herself. The fact was, being back at the farm wasn't going to be all that difficult. When her mother had been dying, and Ella had felt so very isolated, she'd looked forward to the day when she'd get to walk away from the acres that had held her in one place.

What was really causing her to hesitate was the idea of being with Loyal. She liked him. She liked being with him. He, of course, thought of her as nothing more than a sweet, somewhat mousy neighbor.

But she'd always been drawn to him . . . which, of course, meant that there was never going to be anything between them. How could there be?

So, did she really want to spend so much time with him? Was it even wise?

As if she hadn't been standing there, weighing the pros and cons between them for far too long, Loyal prodded. "And so, will you? I'll pick you up at the library and take you over. It will be no trouble."

Oh, it would be no trouble at all. That is, except for her heart.

But wasn't this what she'd been dreaming about? The opportunity to do new things? To push herself? "All right. It is so kind of you."

Pure happiness shone in his eyes. "I am so glad, Ella. Thank you. What time do you get off today?"

"Six o'clock."

"I'll be there then. And I'll have something for dinner, too."

"I'd hate to cause you any trouble."

"It's no trouble. I'm just going to go to the market and get a chicken dinner that's already prepared. If that sounds to your liking?"

"It does. I like the market's chicken just fine." She walked him to the door and smiled at him. "Thank you again."

"I'll see you in a few hours," he promised before putting his hat back on and walking down the short flight of stairs to his buggy.

And though she surely looked foolish, Ella stood on her front stoop and waved goodbye to him as he drove off. A silly, hopeful smile on her face.

"Hey, Graham, what do you know about Mary Zehr?" John asked as they walked to the barn on Friday afternoon. Like usual.

His sister-in-law now had him over one night a week for dinner. John enjoyed the company and the home-cooked meal.

The boys teased John, saying the only reason he was invited over so much was because Katie adored him. He replied that he thought the only reason he was invited was because he gave so much attention to Katie. When she was around her Uncle John, she gave everyone else a break.

Today, he'd volunteered to walk with

Graham to the barn to watch Katie do her chores, which involved feeding and playing with their three rabbits.

As Graham lazily leaned up against the barn's rough wall, chewing on the end of a piece of straw, John stood beside him and grinned. Katie was currently whispering to the rabbits, as though their long ears could hold all her secrets.

"Not much to say about Mary," Graham said after a moment. "She's got a boy named Abel. He's twelve or so."

"I've met Abel. He seems to be a good boy. Mary's told me that he helps out at home and works part-time at the hardware store."

Graham nodded. "He is a mighty hard worker. I feel for him, with the way it's just him and his *mamm*." With a sideways look at John, he said, "When Daed passed on three years ago, it was terribly hard. But at least I was older and had Calvin and Loyal to lean on. Abel is all alone, though."

"Do you think Mary has enough help around her place? A boy can't do everything . . ."

"I haven't heard that she's in need." Graham narrowed his eyes. "Why all the questions?"

"I don't know. She's a nice woman." Okay. Now his collar was starting to feel tight. "Katie, don't forget the rabbits' water."

"It's filled." She twisted her lips. "Kind of."

"That ain't good enough. Rinse it out and give them fresh."

"But—"

"Have a care, Katie," Graham said. "These animals are your responsibility. They are counting on you."

"All right." With a look over her shoulder, she unhooked the water and went to the spigot outside.

John chuckled. "Now I understand why you are standing here with her."

"It's necessary," Graham said with a smile. "But, about Mary, John . . . she's a nice woman. But I thought you were seeing the librarian."

"I am." He cleared his throat. "I mean, I'm seeing her some. It's nothing serious." John fought to keep his voice light and offhand. "I was just curious about Mary, that's all. She's awfully young to be widowed. And she has a lot of responsibility."

"She's not that young. She's Calvin's age."

Now John felt ancient. "I stand corrected."

"Sorry."

"No, it's not your fault I'm touchy about my age. So . . . do you think she had a good marriage? Was her husband a good man?"

"I think so. They were happy." He smiled. "All I really remember about the two of them was when Mary was pregnant. My parents loved to tease William. He would follow Mary everywhere and fuss over her. He was besotted, you know?"

John didn't. He'd never been lucky enough to have a child, but he had the idea that he would be the same way. Aching to protect the woman and baby he loved.

"Uncle John, you're not interested in her, are you?"

He didn't know how he felt. A part of him yearned for Jayne and all the things she represented to him. She was the future he'd always wanted—the woman he'd hoped Angela could be but never was. But Mary, she was the one he found himself thinking about when he was by himself, or when he went to sleep at night. "I might be."

Graham looked at him thoughtfully before watching Katie return with fresh water for the rabbits. "I've always gotten the sense that Mary wasn't the type of woman to take lightly," he finally said.

"I don't intend to." John was saved from having to explain himself when little Katie called out to him.

"Uncle John! Come look at the bunnies! They're hopping all over each other."

"Uh-oh," Graham said. "I'll leave you to that."

Just imagining what was happening, and the explanation he would have to provide to his tiny niece, made him panic. "Graham, you can't leave! Come here and help me."

"No way, *Onkle*. There's a reason we like having you over here so much," he said with a grin. "You give us all a much needed break. See you at supper."

"But—"

Graham waved over his shoulder as he walked away.

"Uncle John, hurry!"

After stepping closer, his suspicion

about what the rabbits were doing was confirmed. "Katie Weaver, you come here and give those rabbits some privacy."

"But—"

Nope. No way was he having this conversation. He was the uncle. The fun guy. Directing her toward the barn, he said, "I heard there's baby chicks. Come show me, sweetheart."

She looked at him and smiled. "I love you, Uncle John."

With a sudden start, John realized that all the confusion he'd been feeling about Jayne and Mary was finally diminishing. Now it seemed that only Mary occupied his thoughts. However, at least he knew where he stood with one special girl in his life.

She was under four feet, as pretty as a picture, and his little buddy.

Chapter 11

Looking out the plate-glass window, Ella once again hoped for a glimpse of Loyal in his buggy. But still, there was no sign of him. She began to get worried. Where could he be?

Doubts settled in. Perhaps Loyal had decided not to come pick her up after all?

Ella craned her neck, looking left again. When yet again she saw no buggy, she felt her stomach knot.

Resolutely, she forced herself to turn around and take a few calming breaths.

Oh, but the nerves were threatening to get the best of her! If the butterflies in her stomach didn't calm down soon, Ella feared she'd be standing all night with her arms wrapped protectively around her middle.

As she was doing now, she realized with a bit of surprise.

Well, this wouldn't do. With effort, she straightened her arms. She needed to get a firm hold of herself, to calm down. It was silly to be so excited. And so nervous!

Of course Loyal wasn't going to forget to come get her.

Of course he wasn't going to change his mind.

"Ella, look at you!" Dorothy proclaimed as she approached the front of the library. "You are certainly ready to leave right on time today."

"*Jah*. I am going—"

"I'm ready, too," Dorothy interrupted. "And guess what? This morning, I thawed out two chicken breasts for supper." As she moved her purse to her other hand, she added, "Why don't you come over as soon as we get home? I'll put the chicken in the oven while you heat up the vege-tables."

"I'm sorry, but I can't have dinner with you tonight."

Dorothy froze. "Whyever not? Are you *grank*?"

"Of course I'm not sick." Ella smiled slightly before once again looking out the window. *Where* was he?

Dorothy's cough claimed her attention once again. "Well then, what are you doing?"

Ella winced. Dorothy's question was loud enough that it had attracted the attention of Ms. Donovan.

And, though she would have preferred to keep her visit with Loyal to herself for just a little bit more, Ella knew there was no sense in trying to hide it. Especially since she'd been standing expectantly at the front windows for the last ten minutes.

"I'm spending some time with Loyal Weaver this evening."

Dorothy's eyebrows rose.

"Loyal is coming here to pick me up," Ella added, crossing her arms over her stomach again.

While Dorothy seemed to be frozen in shock, Ms. Donovan beamed as she came closer. "Is he courting you, Ella? That's exciting news."

"It's surprising," Dorothy muttered.

Ella could practically feel confusion radiating off of Dorothy. Eager to put some space between them, she stepped a bit away from her friend. Then she turned to their boss. "We're not courtin'. It's nothing like that. Loyal and I have been crossing paths lately. When he told me he was redoing the floors, I told him that I thought that was a fine idea." She shrugged. "He offered to show me what the farm looks like this afternoon."

"That sounds very kind of him." Lowering her voice, Jayne confided, "Lately, I've gotten to spend some time with his uncle. John says Loyal is an open and giving person. He says that's a gift Loyal has."

Dorothy frowned. "I don't think he sounds kind at all. In fact, his attention to Ella seems worrisome."

Jayne's eyebrows popped up. "Dorothy, why would you say something like that?"

"Because his motives are surely selfish, of course." Her voice turning louder and more assured, Dorothy added, "I'm sure Loyal Weaver is only showing Ella the farm to make her feel bad." She waved a hand. "After all, what other reason could there be?"

"Because he wants to spend some time with her," her boss countered.

Ella's nervous butterflies had turned into stinging wasps. She hated people discussing her outing in such an open way, as if she wasn't even there! "Loyal is being kind, that's all. We are not courtin'. He's offered to show me the improvements he's been doing on the farm, and I accepted that offer. That is all."

Dorothy crossed her arms over her chest. "If that is all, then I had best make you something to eat for when you get home."

"That's kind of you, but please don't."

"Are you sure? You have to eat—"

"He's bringing dinner," Ella added reluctantly. Now that Dorothy was proving to once again be so controlling, Ella was reluctant to tell her anything more about her plans. "Loyal and I are going to eat there."

Jayne beamed. "It sounds like you're going to have a nice time. Oh, and there he is," she said, pointing to the window.

With a start, Ella glanced toward the street. Indeed, after all this waiting, he'd driven up, and she hadn't even been aware.

Jayne walked to the front door and held

it open. "You better get going, Ella. You don't want to keep him waiting."

Dorothy crossed her arms in front of her. "Yes, we wouldn't want Loyal Weaver to have to wait or be inconvenienced."

Apprehension coursed through her. Something was definitely not right about Dorothy's behavior.

Though it would be uncomfortable, Ella knew it was time to question her friend about her expectations. Never had Ella imagined that she'd be watched and judged like she was.

Unwilling to keep Loyal waiting a moment longer, Ella ignored the heated glare Dorothy was sending her and hurried out the door into the bright, sunny day.

Immediately, the tension in her shoulders lessened with each step toward Loyal's buggy.

He stepped out and walked around to her side. He was dressed in a crisp white shirt and black pants with suspenders.

But none of those things could hold a candle to the glow in his eyes. They sparkled with happiness. Warming her insides, sending all the nerves and misgivings away.

"Good afternoon, Ella," he said with a slight nod.

"Good afternoon to you. Thank you for picking me up. I hope it wasn't too much trouble?"

One strong hand grasped her elbow as she stepped into the buggy. "This was no trouble at all," he said. "As a matter of fact, I've been looking forward to this all day."

Ella swallowed hard as he walked around to his side and hopped in beside her.

As he pulled off his hat and pushed back his hair, he started telling her about his day—and Ella smiled brightly at him. The fact was, she liked Loyal. She liked him a lot. And even if they could be no more than just friends, for now it would be enough.

She was bound and determined to finally live her life. After twenty-four years of waiting, the time had come.

Chapter 12

This was probably a bad idea, Loyal thought as he motioned for Beauty to move forward. He'd been excited to share the improvements he'd been making to her old house; had thought that there was surely no one else who would appreciate the changes so well.

But now that she sat next to him, he began to doubt his idea. Perhaps taking Ella to her former home was a bit like rubbing salt into a wound?

When he glanced behind him, he noticed two women standing in front of one of the large windows at the front of the library. One wore a benevolent smile while the taller woman's glare was stern enough to freeze the hardiest of constitutions. "I guess your leaving with me didn't escape anyone's notice?"

After turning her head to the library again, Ella looked back his way and frowned. "I'm afraid not. That's Ms. Donovan and Dorothy."

Though he knew the taller woman was Dorothy Zook, he'd never had much of a willingness to talk to her. She was older but, more than that, had a reputation for being especially dour.

"Ms. Donovan is the librarian, right?" Vaguely he recalled his uncle mentioning her.

"*Jah*. She's rather new to Jacob's Crossing. She's mighty kind."

Ella's lips were set in a fine line. Actually, Loyal realized that with each block they passed, she seemed more and more perturbed. Finally he decided to be as direct as possible. "Ella, are you having doubts about visiting the farm tonight? I hadn't thought about it, but now I'm guessing it might be uncomfortable, stopping by a place that has so many memories. I would be happy to take you home if you are."

Panic lit her eyes. "I'm not having doubts."

"All right, then," he said as he pulled the reins and worked the buggy's break as they approached a red light. When they were stopped, he glanced her way again. Just to notice that she'd already been looking at him.

Ella's cheeks pinkened.

And Loyal's spirits rose. *Hmm* . . . Perhaps it wasn't worries about her house that was occupying her thoughts.

Little by little, as the tiny town square faded from view, Ella seemed to relax. Soon the few cars they shared the road with passed them, and the quiet stillness of the country evening embraced them.

Ella crossed her legs and finally leaned back against the back of the bench. Now they were merely six or seven inches apart. When she'd first sat down, she seemed to hug the edge of the bench. So much so, that Loyal had been worried her skirts would be blowing out the opening of the buggy.

The silence stretched between them, but the tension eased, turning companionable. Loyal became aware of the scent of roses . . . she must have used a rose-scented shampoo or lotion.

He was just about to point out a fall display of mums in front of a farm when she spoke. "Loyal, Dorothy's behavior is concerning me."

Glad she was trusting him enough to share what was on her mind, he glanced her way. "Why? What is she doing??"

She bit her lip, then spoke. "She's becoming possessive."

"I don't understand."

"Well, see, I've known her for quite some time. When my father passed away, she stopped by often. And, over the last year, she's been coming by regularly to give me company while my mother fought her disease."

Loyal felt yet another burst of guilt. Though he knew his mother had stopped by every so often, he'd never even considered paying Ella a call. Actually, he hadn't spared a thought about her feelings.

All he'd cared about was that she would put her farm up for auction. Sooner than later.

"She was a *gut* friend," he murmured. His behavior, on the other hand, was shameful.

"Oh, Dorothy was," she said quickly. "Though we didn't see eye to eye on everything, I've counted myself very blessed to have her." With a wary glance in his direction, she said, "It's difficult to be alone, day after day."

"I imagine it is."

"Anyway, after my mother passed, Dorothy helped me get the library job, and she owns the duplex I am living in." She darted another wary, uncertain glance his way. "Obviously, I owe her a lot."

He had a bit of an idea about where her thoughts were heading. "Friendship is never one-sided, Ella. I'm sure Dorothy was glad to be able to help you. Giving sometimes makes a person feel as good as taking, don't you think?"

"Thank you for saying that."

"I'm not just saying it, it's true. Why do you say she's now acting peculiar?"

"She constantly watches me. Expects me to be with her all day long."

"I don't have much experience with that, but with my brothers, sometimes we take each other for granted. There's been times when I've just assumed Calvin will help me with a chore, or Graham will accompany me to the market."

"*Nee,* this is different."

Loyal racked his brain a bit more. It was kind of enjoyable getting to hear someone else's problems and being asked for advice. "Perhaps it's just a case of too much togetherness? Sometimes, no matter how much you care for a person, a little space is a nice change of pace." He smiled. "I've felt that way a time or two, you know. It's one of the reasons I was anxious to purchase your farm."

She smiled slightly, letting him know that she wasn't upset about being reminded of his purchase. "Loyal, you make a good point, but I don't know. See, I thought it might take some getting used to, living in town and working, but those things have been a real joy to me. It's far harder to be alone on a farm with only your thoughts for days on end."

She sighed. "But it is Dorothy's attitude that is proving to be a trial." After a pause, she said, "Dorothy seems almost jealous, Loyal. If I don't want to eat every meal with her, or walk with her in the morning, she gets visibly upset."

He was drawn into the story in spite of his original goal just to be a good listener. "Jealous how?"

"She turns angry. Glares at me. She makes cutting comments."

"My word."

Ella nodded. "She's jealous of my time, and even seems to be jealous of you. She was not happy I was going to see the farm with you this evening. She'd planned for us to have dinner together. But, Loyal, we hadn't even discussed dinner. She just assumed that I wouldn't have anything else to do." Clearing her throat, she added, "She couldn't believe I'd rather do this with you."

He felt his cheeks color. Had Ella completely mistaken his attentions? Stumbling over his words, he said, "I only wanted to show you the farm . . . to show you the wood floors . . ."

"Oh! Oh, of course! I haven't misunderstood a thing!" she blurted, resting her hand on his arm. "I know you are just taking me to see the farm out of kindness. But I'm afraid Dorothy doesn't see it that way."

Her hand still clung to his forearm. Holding him.

How could four fingers leave such an impression on him? He was as aware of her hand as he was of her words. And of the array of feelings flowing through him.

Loyal struggled to sound merely concerned. Friend-like. "And how does Dorothy see it?"

"Like you're being cruel."

That stunned him. "I don't understand."

As if she'd just realized she'd been clinging to him, Ella pulled her hand away. Rested it on her lap. "I didn't, either. But when I asked her to explain herself, Dorothy said that she was sure you just wanted to rub your ownership in."

"That's not who I am," he said indignantly. "Ella, that never entered my mind."

"I know. At least, I didn't think it had." She shook her head. "I'm sorry I even brought this up. I shouldn't be talking about her, and I surely shouldn't be talking about her to you."

"Why not me? It is my motivations and actions that are being commented on."

"And that is wrong. I guess I was just attempting to explain her interest. The reason she was watching us out the window with a scowl." More quietly, she added, "And why I was first so tense when I joined you. I didn't want you to be upset with me, Loyal."

"I'm not upset. Please don't be sorry. I'm glad you are sharing this with me." And to his surprise, Loyal realized that he meant every word. He wanted to be a person she could lean on. He wanted to be her friend.

She raised an eyebrow. "You're glad I'm pouring out all my worries to you?"

"If it makes you feel better, I am." Feeling self-conscious, he added, "I must say, Ella, if I were you, I'd worry a bit about being too close to Dorothy. She sounds like the type of person who isn't afraid to cause trouble."

"I'm beginning to think you might be right."

Unable to help himself, Loyal reached out and squeezed her hand. Wanting to reassure her with a simple touch. "I'm glad you talked to me. Do so, anytime."

"I hate to burden you . . ."

"I don't mind." Taking a hold of the reins with both hands again, he let his words sink in as they drove the last few minutes out to the farm. The slight breeze cooled his skin, and there was the faint scent of a fire burning in the distance.

He smiled, enjoying the first scent of fall.

Little by little, the tension between them eased. He pointed out red leaves on a maple. She laughed at a squirrel scurrying by, his mouth full of acorn.

Loyal grinned and shared a story about some of the animals on his farm. "Katie is no match for the chickens," he said. "I hope she learns to be as bossy with the hens as she is with the rest of us."

Ella's eyes lit up. "Speaking of your sister . . . I have to tell you that I'm enjoying your dear sister *verra* much. She's a mighty sweet girl."

"She's sweet, and a lot of other things, too," he said, glad she'd moved to a lighter topic. "She took a shine to you, I have to say. We all heard about how much she enjoyed your story. And about how much she is looking forward to the reading club."

Ella beamed. For the rest of their journey, she chattered about the reading club and the prizes that could be earned and about his sister.

When she talked about books and the children, her eyes lit up, and all the worry and tenseness that seemed to character-ize her drifted away.

Suddenly, she wasn't just mousy Ella with the too-thick glasses and the curly brown hair. Loyal began to see that there was a sweet sense of humor resting under-neath. And that her dark brown eyes were framed by thick, long eyelashes.

And that her nose was dusted with freck-les. And that her smile was pretty, too.

It was like she'd suddenly become so much more than the woman he'd always taken for granted.

With some relief, he parked the buggy in front of the house. "We're here."

"Oh, yes. We are," she practically shouted, scooting out of the buggy in a hurry. As if she couldn't wait to feel the fa-miliar dirt underneath her feet.

Loyal got out of the buggy at a far slower pace. Hoping to control his reaction to her.

Here, in her old home, Ella showed him yet another facet of herself. Here, Ella positively glowed.

She turned to him, all smiles and giddi-ness. "Can we go right inside? I can't wait to see how the floors look. And then, when we're done, perhaps we could eat outside? Over by that tall oak is a wonderful-*gut* place to picnic." She bit her lip. "Is that all right with you? I don't want to step on your toes . . ."

"My toes are fine, Ella," he said, unable to help himself from grinning.

She smiled, too. Right before she opened the door and charged inside, chattering like a schoolgirl. Sounding young and fresh and adorable.

Slightly stunned, all Loyal could do was follow. And think that once again, Ella Hostetler was more than he'd ever imagined.

Chapter 13

It was hard being Katie Weaver. Not a person in the whole house was giving her any mind and she'd sure tried to get them to listen. "But why can't I walk over to see Loyal? You've walked there by yourself."

"For the same reason we told you ten minutes ago," Lucy said. "It's too far for a little girl to go. Plus, I would worry about you."

"You could come with me. If you did, then I wouldn't be alone."

"Katie, you know I cannot. I'm cooking supper."

"But I really want to go."

"You should be helping me prepare our meal, don't you think?"

Katie bit her lip. That was the problem with Lucy, she decided. Lucy always did the right thing. She was so good that Katie knew she could never be so perfect.

Especially since, most of the time, the right thing sounded like the boring thing.

Before Lucy actually gave her a task, Katie tugged on her eldest brother's sleeve. "Calvin, come on. Please?"

But though he usually had more patience with her than anyone, Calvin frowned. "Katie, you need to mind your manners. Lucy told you no. You're being far too bossy."

She was only being called bossy because no one else liked what she was saying. "I am minding my manners."

"Barely," Calvin murmured. "You need to learn to accept when you don't get your way."

She didn't get her way a lot.

But no one understood just how much she wanted to go to Loyal's farm. In desperation, she turned to Graham. "Graham? Please?"

Patting her on the head, he said, "So, you're now desperate enough to ask me?"

"Jah." Her cheeks heated, and she squirmed under Graham's teasing stare. But she couldn't deny it. There wasn't really any reason to lie, was there?

"Katie!" her mother called out from her spot in front of the sink. "Your tongue is too sharp by half this evening. Enough. If you don't stop being such a pest, I'm going to send you straight to your room."

Katie winced. More than anything, she hated to sit by herself in her room. Tears pricked her eyes as she tried to tell herself not to push any more.

But with giving in came a lump of frustration deep inside. "Mamm, I know you want me to be a good girl, and I really do try."

"Then why do you keep asking us to take you to see Loyal?" Calvin asked. "You know he's working."

"He's not. Miss Ella is there."

Around her, the whole kitchen stilled. Graham grinned. "Really? Tell us more, Katie."

"Loyal stopped by here earlier and told me Miss Ella was going to visit his farm tonight. But, see, Miss Ella said next time we saw each other, she would talk to me about my books. And I loved reading them. And now she's so close, and no one has any time to take me to the library, and I'm too small to go by myself."

Stunned silence met her long stream of words. Feeling so frustrated, Katie swallowed hard and tried not to cry. If she cried, she was sure her mother was going to think she was crying on purpose, just to get her way.

But that wasn't what she was doing. She just wanted to see Ella.

But instead of joining in with the criticism, Graham chuckled. "Come here, child," he murmured, picking her up and popping her on his lap. "You probably won't believe this, but I understand your feelings. I, too, was once the youngest. It's hard, ain't it?"

Katie nodded.

Lifting her chin with one finger, he looked her in the eye. "I'd take you, but it's not the right thing to do. We can't simply invite ourselves over to Loyal's farm."

"Why not? He's still our *bruder*. . . . He loves us."

"I know he does, but he might not care to be disturbed. After all, this is his special time with Ella."

"But you all told me they were just friends. And I want to tell her that I finished my third book."

With a weary expression, her mother looked at Graham. "Supper won't be ready for another hour. Perhaps you could go with Katie over there? I have a canning party tomorrow and so I won't be able to take her to the library then. This might be her only chance to see Ella. Katie, can you be good and not a pest?"

"Yes." She almost said more but caught Graham's fingers pretending to lock his lips. It was her reminder to leave well enough alone.

"All right, then. Go now."

"Are you ready, Kit Kat?"

Katie sighed in relief. Graham only called her that name when he was happy with her. "I am."

"Then let's go."

Just as they were walking out the door, she heard Calvin ask if any of them had been as much of a handful as she was.

Though a protest was filling her brain, Graham rested his hand on her shoulder again. "Patience and peace, Katie. You've gotten your way. That's enough."

Her lips curving upward; she supposed Graham had a point.

Ella would have never imagined she would be comfortable eating a picnic dinner beside Loyal Weaver. Always too plain and too shy, she'd never been the type of girl who boys had flirted with or courted.

Then, of course, she was so isolated while taking care of her mother. She'd been occupied with that when other girls her age were going for walks and buggy rides with eligible men.

And picnic suppers, too.

But for all that, the main reason she hadn't ever thought she could sit with Loyal comfortably was because he was, well, Loyal Weaver.

For most of her life, it was as if the two of them had lived in separate spheres. There'd never been any animosity between them, just nothing in common.

Loyal was the middle son of a well-off family in good standing in their community. In school, he'd been the most talkative of his brothers. He also had an easy way about him that had been contagious. People were instantly charmed by his quick wit and laugh.

And his lovely blue eyes and handsome appearance didn't hurt his popularity, either.

In contrast, Ella was shyer, and her looks had never been much to comment on. While she knew she wasn't exactly homely, her appearance was just the type to blend in, not stand out. Until recently, that distinction had suited her fine. She was the dutiful daughter, dependent on her mother's needs. Spending much of her time alone.

Until Loyal had bought her family's farm, the majority of their interaction had come from brief conversations after church. If that.

And now, here she was, sitting across from him on a quilt, eating roasted chicken and cornbread on her lap, and laughing about pigs. Pigs!

"Honestly, Ella, deciding not to raise pigs had to be the best decision you ever made. When we had a pair years ago, I grew to hate going to the animals' pens."

She couldn't help but be charmed. "Because of their smell?"

"Most definitely. But also because of the fact that they are jealous animals. The female sow was in love with Graham. She followed him everywhere that she could—and once broke down a fence trying to get his attention."

"And what did Graham think about that?"

"About what you would imagine, of course! He wanted Daed to butcher her immediately."

Ella laughed. "That poor *pikk*. Good men are hard to come by. I bet your sow knew Graham was a catch."

"All Graham knew was that he had enough troubles without a wandering pig added to the mix." The corners of Loyal's eyes crinkled. "It is funny now, because it was so long ago."

"Time always does heal wounds, yes?" she said softly.

Removing his plate from his lap, he shifted. "Are you doing all right, Ella? Living in a new place, away from all the memories?"

"I'm doing better than I imagined I would." After mentally weighing whether or not to tell him any more personal stories, she shrugged. "In some ways, I think my *mamm* has been gone to me for some time. She'd been weakened by her kidney ailments and by my father's passing. I'm afraid she looked forward to death."

"That's hard to live with."

"It was." She waved a hand. "All this land was a blessing. But at times it was a curse, too. I've been separated out here from most everything."

"I'm sorry. When my father passed on to heaven, at first we worried about my mother's disposition. But then, of course, Katie refused to be ignored."

The air between them warmed, but not from heat. Instead, it came from the new way they were able to speak to each other. The new understanding that was forming. . . . A bond.

Now it seemed possible for them to one day be true friends. And though, in the middle of the night, Ella might know she wished for more than that, here on the grass she was enough of a realist to understand that a romance between her and Loyal was unlikely.

She was a year older than he and as far financially as was possible. And, then, of course, there were the obvious differences. He was Loyal Weaver, the darling of their town. Everyone's favorite.

She was not.

When his story was finished, she laughed and was just about to ask him to tell her more about his family when they noticed Graham and Katie riding up on a horse.

Ella looked at Loyal in confusion. "Did you know they were coming?" she asked.

"Not at all," he replied, getting to his feet. Though he didn't look upset, he didn't look particularly pleased, either.

Loyal quickly stepped to the side as Katie rumbled past him and skidded to a stop a mere eight inches from Ella's knees. "Katie, watch yourself," he cautioned. "You just about ran over Ella."

It was obvious Katie tried to look contrite, but it was also obvious that she wasn't very regretful at all. "I was afraid we were going to miss you," she said, taking a look in Graham's direction almost spitefully. "I've been trying all afternoon to come see you."

Finally reaching them, Graham shook his head. "*Nee,* she only recently decided that she had to come here. And she was near as difficult as could be until I volunteered to ride over here with you." He grunted. "Which you still have not thanked me for, I might add."

"Danke."

Loyal would've reprimanded Katie for her lack of manners one more time—except that Ella was grinning like a Cheshire cat. "You wanted to come see your brother, child?" she said, bending down a bit so they were almost eye to eye.

"She misses me," Loyal said.

Katie looked up at him and frowned. "But I didn't come to see you. I came to see Ella."

Graham winked his way. "If ever you need someone to make you feel unimportant, Katie is the one to pick."

Embarrassed, because somehow Ella's smile had grown broader, Loyal said, "Obviously."

"Why did you want to see us?" Ella asked. "Did you have a question about the farm?"

Katie shook her head. "I wanted to tell you about my books."

"Katie! That is something you could have done another time."

"No, I couldn't have. Miss Ella knows all about books. And she gave me a chart," she added in a rush.

"She was really excited about it," Graham said.

Loyal closed his mouth. He knew exactly what his brother had been dealing with. Katie on a mission to get her way was surely a force to be reckoned with.

"Come here, child, and sit with me." Hesitantly, Ella also looked toward Graham. "We were just having a picnic, but Loyal bought a lot of food. There's more than enough to share. Would you like to have some chicken?"

Graham eyed the food like a man who'd been without any for days. "Do you mind, brother?"

Ella stared at Loyal warily.

"Of course not." Now that he wasn't irritated with his sister, he was finally seeing the humor in the situation. Of course Katie would find a way to nose her way into anything members of the family were involved in. That was her way.

Katie edged closer to Ella and opened up the satchel she'd just noticed that Katie was carrying over her shoulder.

And Ella—after a quick glance Loyal's way—leaned forward and ooed and aahed over the little girl's accomplishments.

For a quick second, he stared at her and thought she was the prettiest woman he'd ever seen. The realization was sharp and unexpected. And definitely true.

Chapter 14

The sky was turning dark and the stars were coming out when Loyal took her home. As the buggy clip-clopped along the paved roads, a faint breeze fanned Ella's face. Now that it was mid-August, the breeze was tinged with a pinch of cold.

Oh, she was so ready for the change of season.

As Loyal parked the buggy in front of her home, his horse pranced a bit. "Beauty, settle now," he said.

Ella looked at his gelding and couldn't help but smile. "Unlike me, that *gaul* still has got energy to spare."

Loyal chuckled. "*Nah*. This is just his way of telling me that he's had enough walking for the day. He's a lazy horse and an early-to-bed kind of man. Here it is, almost nine. He's ready to be settled for the night. Once he gets in his stall at home, he'll be as docile as a lamb."

Stepping out of the buggy, Ella stretched her arms to her side. "I might have more in common with Beauty than I thought. I'm an early-to-bed kind of woman."

Loyal followed her out, shaking one of his legs as though he was hoping to restore its circulation. "Most likely, we all are."

As he stood next to her, Ella became even more aware of his size and proximity. She was tall, but he was at least four inches taller. Most likely a little over six feet. His posture was as relaxed and easy as ever; his muscular frame as solid and sturdy. Next to him, she felt comfortable and almost petite.

Once again, their eyes met, and the sweet link that had formed between them grew warmer. Little by little, her cheeks heated. Ella hoped the fading light hid rather than accentuated her blooming color. "I had a wonderful-*gut* time tonight," she said formally. "And the house—it looks good."

His gaze warmed. "I'm glad seeing it didn't make you melancholy."

"I had thought it might, but instead it just reminds me of all the work there was to do," she replied, meaning every word. "The floors look nice, and the painted kitchen does, too. It was kind of you to show it to me."

"I'm glad you came." Waving her forward, he said, "I'll walk you inside."

Now that the last of the sunlight had faded into the horizon, it seemed as if there was no one around but the two of them.

And perhaps there wasn't, she reflected, almost dreamily. Perhaps they were the only two people on the sidewalk in Jacob's Crossing. The last two people reluctant to say good night.

Oh, but she was such a silly old maid, dreaming such things. "There's no need," she said in a rush. "I'll be fine."

"It's dark out and you're here in the middle of town . . ." He frowned. "Perhaps

I should walk with you through your apartment? Just to make sure everything there is as it should be?"

"It's what I need to get used to, yes? I'll be fine."

Hurriedly, she strode to the steps and stepped up the first two. Just to illustrate her point. *"Gut nacht,* Loyal."

His gaze skimmed over her face. *"Gut nacht,"* he echoed, then turned and got back into the buggy.

She watched him until he picked up the reins, then turned and quickly climbed the last three steps and unlocked her door.

As Beauty's hooves faded into the distance, Ella felt a shiver of foreboding and wished for a moment that she hadn't tried to act so brave.

Truthfully, it was terribly dark inside. She left the door open as she crossed to the table next to her reading chair and lit the kerosene light. It was probably her imagination, but her footsteps seemed overly loud.

As the soft, golden glow illuminated the room, Ella closed the door and locked it.

No windows were open, of course. The

room was stuffy and too warm. Perspiration ran in a trickle down her back, making the fabric of her dress stick to her skin like glue. Eager to feel cooler, she opened the front window a good four inches, then walked to her bedroom and opened the two windows there even wider. Instantly a fresh breeze fluttered the plain white curtains and fanned her face.

Next she sat on the edge of her bed and carefully removed her black bonnet, then removed her shoes and stockings. Ah, freedom! Giving into temptation, she flopped backward on the bed, just enjoying the sensation of the cool breezes floating across her skin and the delicious feeling of wiggling bare toes that had been confined in black stockings and shoes for too many hours.

A yawn encouraged her to hop up and begin her nightly chores.

She walked back to the kitchen, eager to make tea. The feel of the planks of wood under her feet made her think of Loyal's hard work. Her old house really would look far better, now that the old musty carpet was gone.

To her surprise, while there, she hadn't felt any of resentment or loss, the kind she had been sure she would experience when leaving the farm. Instead, she'd felt only a mild interest, and later was filled with a hint of excitement as she noticed Loyal's excitement.

Katie's and Graham's presence had helped, too. Katie's happiness to visit with her was flattering, Graham's steady humor had made any uncomfortable sensations she might have felt fall by the wayside.

They'd created a nice buffer between her and Loyal, too. She didn't feel as much pressure to say the right things when they were around.

She hadn't been away long enough to forget how much work everything had been. When she'd looked at the garden, Ella only thought about how tired and sore she'd been when it had been time to weed, harvest, and can nature's bounty.

She now noticed how the barn and fencing desperately needed a new coat of paint, that the kitchen sink needed a new faucet; and recalled that windows in the front room always stuck.

In contrast, here everything worked fine. And because of its size, she could now make a cup of hot tea, take a quick shower, and then enjoy some time with her nose in a book before going to sleep.

Still turning over the night's events in her mind, Ella filled her kettle and lit a burner. As the water heated, a note on the counter caught her attention.

A prickle of unease skittered down her spine. She didn't recall putting anything there. Crossing the small area, she picked it up and realized it was a neatly folded sheet of notebook paper. Warily, she unfolded the paper, still doing her best to remember when she might have set the paper there.

Trying still to recall when she would have written anything on the paper or from where she would have picked it up, she realized that, but of course, she hadn't done either. She didn't write herself notes and didn't leave important papers scattered on the kitchen counters.

As she smoothed the creases from the page and noticed the handwriting, the paper's appearance all made sense.

It made sense, but it certainly didn't alleviate her worries. No, if anything, solving the mystery only served to increase the tension in her body.

For some reason, Dorothy had come into her apartment and placed the note there. That very evening.

As the kettle whistled, Ella removed the pot from the burner and poured the water into her awaiting cup. Immediately, the soothing tang of chamomile wafted upward. She added a pinch of sugar, then took the mug and the letter to her favorite chair.

All of a sudden, hot tea and the familiar comfort of her favorite chair felt like lifelines. Shifting a bit, she tucked her feet up under her thighs, struggling to ward off the sudden chill she felt.

After a day of being too warm and complaining about the humidity and heat, now she felt chilled to the bone.

Focusing her eyes, she read the page.

Ella. I feel I should let you know it is now after eight. You really should be home by now. Once more, you shouldn't have gone anywhere with Loyal Weaver.

He is not to be trusted. And if you trust him, I will be disappointed in you.

Ella, if you're not careful, your reputation will get ruined, and I'll be forced to ask you to leave. Don't make me do that.

Because no matter how badly you treat me, I will always be there for you. I put your half of our dinner in your refrigerator. I hope you will enjoy it.

Tonight, when you say your prayers, I hope you'll ask for forgiveness. The way you're treating me is shameful. After all, I am the only one who has always been your friend. I'm the only one who will stay your friend, long after everyone else moves on and leaves you.

You should remember that.

With a shaking hand, Ella put the note down. Shock and anger mixed inside of her. As soon as possible, she was going to need to talk with Dorothy. Her friend must have completely misunderstood Ella's intentions when she'd moved to the duplex.

Surely, as soon as they discussed everything and cleared the air, things would be just fine between them. After all, they had to be. Where else could she go?

Chapter 15

Mattie couldn't deny how ugly she felt. It had been terribly difficult to have no hair, and even harder to get used to the fuzz that now covered her scalp.

And harder still to accept her looks and go out in public this way. Though she'd never been especially shy, she didn't like how different she looked, and how those differences caused others to look at her curiously.

It was far easier to stay home, away from strangers' eyes. Away even from the concerned expressions of the folks in her community.

However, during one of her last visits to the hospital, a social worker talked to her about her feelings.

"You have a choice, Mattie," she'd said. "You can either hide until you are perfect again, or face the facts that none of us are that way and move on."

The lady's matter-of-fact tone had grated on her nerves. "You think it's that easy?" she'd asked.

"I know it's not that easy at all," the counselor replied. "I think facing the world as a cancer survivor might be one of the hardest things a person ever has to do. But I have to tell you that many a man and woman have told me that only staring at four walls inside a house can be difficult, too." With a shooing motion, she added, "You can't hide what the drugs did to you, dear. So you might as well embrace the side effects, yes?"

"I don't know—"

"Give it a try, and then come back next week and talk to me."

"You wouldn't mind?"

"Not at all. We're a full-service hospital here. Go, and then report back to me."

Bolstered by the woman's encouragement, Mattie decided to ask Corrine to be by her side for her first outing. Corrine was easy to be with and took things in stride.

When Corrine suggested they go to the Kaffi Haus, Mattie readily agreed. Loyal's Uncle John owned the shop and so it seemed like a safe place to go.

When Mattie got to the corner of Jacob's Crossing's square, Corrine was waiting for her. "I'm so glad we're first going to the donut shop," Mattie said. "I don't get enough of a chance to come over here. Nothing sounded good while I was getting treatments. Now I seem to be eating double the amount I used to."

"You're still too skinny." Corrine linked Mattie's hand through her elbow. "We'll have to do this all the time. Of course, then I'll get fat."

Mattie looked over Corrine's frame and shook her head. "You're perfect the way you are, Corrine. I wouldn't want you any other way."

As their walk continued, Mattie slowly felt the muscles in her shoulders relax, and little by little she lifted her chin a bit.

Things even got easier when they

entered John Weaver's Kaffi Haus and an impromptu cheer rang out.

"Mattie Lapp! Aren't you a sight for sore eyes."

Mattie walked over and hugged Mrs. Miller. "It's *gut* to see you as well."

"And how are you feeling?"

"Better." She faltered for something more to say but drew a blank. This was becoming a common occurrence. Her brain and body felt muddled—perhaps it was a side effect from the medicines?

"I'm practically starving," Corrine said, grabbing Mattie's arm and pulling her forward. "Let's eat."

Once they were sitting down, sipping coffee, and enjoying two jelly-filled pastries, Corrine lowered her voice. "So, how are you doing, really?"

Though she still felt like she was deep in the middle of a void, Mattie shrugged. "I'm doing better. I mean, better than I was," she amended.

"That good, hmm?"

"There's no need for sarcasm, Corrine. Some days are better than ever. Some days are worse."

"That's a shame."

"It is. But it's also the truth. I'll take that."

"Well, yes. I suppose the truth is all we can ask for." She paused, making Mattie anxious. The last thing she wanted to do was face another round of questions about her health. She didn't mind talking about herself, but surely there was more to her than her cancer?

After finishing off her lemon donut, Corrine sighed dramatically, even going so far as to stretch her hands out in front of her. "Mattie Lapp, I'm ashamed of you."

"Why?"

"We've spent all this time together, and not once have you asked me about my garden."

"How could I have forgotten? What is new?"

"A lot." Leaning forward, her face became even more animated. "Have I told you about the battle I've waged between a pair of rabbits and my strawberries?"

"You have not. What is going on?"

"A pair of rabbits have taken to eating all my berries."

"That's to be expected . . ."

"Perhaps. But what is not expected is that they're eating just one bite of each!"

That startled a laugh from Mattie. "Corrine, surely not."

She held up her hand. "It's the truth. I promise it is. And it's enough to make me cry, I tell you that."

"So what have you been doing?"

"They come at twilight, so Peter and I have been waiting for them and then scaring them off!"

"Corrine. Set a trap."

"We tried that, but they got away. They're wily rabbits, I tell ya."

Mattie's eyes started tearing up, she was laughing so hard. "Never say that you and Peter have nothing to do at night." After a pause, Corrine started laughing, too.

They were giggling so much, they almost missed the next arrivals: Jenna Yoder, followed by Loyal Weaver.

While Loyal merely acknowledged them, then went to go sit at the counter with the other men, Jenna smiled their way, got herself a coffee, and sat down with them.

"Mattie, I didn't know you were doing so well."

While Mattie knew Jenna's words weren't meant to sound critical, she felt herself tense up. Jenna was a pretty girl—tall, slim, and blessed with rich golden-colored hair and eyes that were a beautiful mix of green and blue. In contrast, Mattie felt more conspicuous than ever. "I'm doing better," she finally said. "I'm done with chemotherapy and radiation treatments. Actually, I'm down to just a few pills a day."

"Better than that," Corrine said supportively. "She's able to eat out sometimes now."

"That is a blessing. Why, last time I went riding with Graham, all he said about you was that you were still *shvach*."

"I am still weak," she allowed, then stopped, at a loss of what else to say.

The tense sensation in her stomach was evolving into something more taut and bitter as each second passed. Graham was only her friend. That was true. Never had she ever considered him in a romantic sense.

So why was she suddenly wishing that Jenna and he would not be getting along?

Jenna got to her feet. "I'd truly love to sit with you two some more, but I suppose I should go sit with Loyal now."

Corrine raised a brow. "He's at the counter with the men."

"But I don't want him to think I'm ignoring him, since I've been seeing so much of his brother, you know." Jenna turned and walked away before either Corrine or Mattie could comment.

But her quick exit didn't stop them from watching Jenna approach Loyal and the play of confused expressions on his face when he realized she intended to sit with him.

Corrine nudged Mattie with her foot. "Loyal is your neighbor, Mattie. Do you think you should go over there, too, just so he won't think you're ignoring him?"

Mattie giggled under her breath. Oh, but she did love Corrine's feisty sense of humor! She was about to say something else when Loyal scooted off his stool and headed for the door, his Styrofoam cup in one hand and a bag of donuts in the other.

Then, just like they were watching a children's play, they watched him quickly cross the parking lot, scamper across the road, and stride over to Ella Hostetler. After a brief conversation, the two of them started walking together. Ella talking and Loyal smiling at her.

Just like he didn't want to be anywhere

else in the world. "Now, isn't that interesting?" Mattie wondered aloud.

"Almost as interesting as watching Jenna sitting quietly at the counter with a line of men," Corrine whispered. "I hope she starts chatting with them soon . . . or they'll think they're being ignored!"

All at once, Mattie's terrible knot of nerves dissipated and true, warm, and easy feelings flowed through her.

They lasted all day. Right up to that evening. When she felt a lump under her armpit.

Chapter 16

Just a block from her house, Loyal held up his white sack and hoped he didn't look too desperate. "I've got donuts. Do you have time to have one before work?"

A whole wealth of expressions crossed Ella's face. So much so, that Loyal felt he was getting a front-row seat into her mind as confusion, pleasure, and hope flashed before him.

It was that look of hope that made him smile a bit more brightly. "I hope you can spare me a few minutes," he added.

"Sure. That sounds fine," she said finally.

That sounds fine? For a moment there, she'd looked like she was about to tell him something of great importance. "There's a bench about a block from here, off to the side. Do you want to go there?"

"*Jah.* I would like that."

That was not the response he'd been hoping for.

Loyal stepped to Ella's side and walked beside her on the sidewalk, waiting for a friendly smile. But whatever he'd thought was between them seemed to have disappeared. Was she no longer interested in him? "Is something the matter?" he finally asked after they'd gone halfway and she'd kept her lips tightly shut. "Are you upset with me for some reason?"

She darted a glance his way. "Not at all."

"I guess I was mistaken."

With another glance, her lips curved into a smile. "I suppose I deserved that, didn't I? I'm sorry. I'm a bit distracted, and a little worried about something."

"If you'd care to share, I bet I can help."

She tilted her head up to him as they stopped under the welcome shade of a maple. "It's nothing." She bit her lip as indecision crossed her face again. "Well, maybe talking about things might help . . ."

Though it was a little forward, he took her arm, guided her to the bench, and sat beside her. "What do you want to talk about? Are you having trouble with your new job?"

"Oh, no. It's a wonderful-*gut* job. As you know." She shook her head with a smile. "That Katie, she makes me laugh, she does."

"Ella, though we have Katie now, I basically grew up with boys. We don't beat around the bush when we have something on our minds. What is the matter?"

She inhaled deeply. "Someone told me that it makes no sense for you to want to spend time with me. And now, when I think about it, I suppose that is true."

"You've lost me. Why wouldn't I want to spend time with you?"

Her foot started tapping. Loyal watched her black shoe beat a staccato rhythm, getting faster and louder until it made him grit his teeth.

It took everything he had not to step on her toes to put an end to it. "Ella? Please?"

"I'm older than you," she finally said in a rush.

"By one year. That hardly counts. Is that the big problem?"

"Not exactly."

"Ella . . ."

"Oh . . . all right. It's also this," she said, waving a hand over herself.

Concentrating, he looked hard at her dress, but for the life of him, he didn't notice anything special about it. Panic set in.

He'd heard girls liked men to notice things about them. Special things, like new dresses. "Is your *rokk* new?" he asked, hoping he'd guessed right.

"Of course not."

"Oh." Feeling remarkably dumb, he took another look at it. All he noticed about it was that it was gray. And looked pretty much like every other woman's dress. Seeing that she was waiting for some specific pronouncement, Loyal swallowed. "Um. It's a right fine dress?"

"Oh, Loyal. I'm not talking about the dress, I'm talking about me."

Now panic was really settling in. He had no idea about how to respond to that. She was just . . . Ella. "What about you?"

"Come, now. You know."

"I don't. Aren't we talking in circles now?"

"All right. I've got glasses. And thick brown hair." She wrinkled her nose. "And I'm tall, too."

"I know."

"Loyal, I'm not petite at all. And I've got big feet." Softly, she repeated, "I'm not small at all."

While it was true he used to think of her as *Plain Ella,* now Loyal thought about her far differently. He liked that she was almost as tall as him. And that she didn't look as if she'd break if she went for a long walk . . . or if he gave her a hug. Actually, he had thought she'd fit quite nicely in his arms.

And her hair? He liked it. His hair was a shade darker than his brother's wife's hair—but even Lucy's caramel-blond color didn't seem as rich and vibrant as Ella's.

He almost laughed off her concerns. Truthfully, they sounded so silly. But then, he noticed a hesitation in her eyes and rethought his decision. "I've never minded your height. And your feet, well, I imagine that God decided you needed feet the size they are in order to support your frame."

When he finished, he smiled in satisfaction.

But she didn't smile back. "Loyal. . . . Truly, that's all you think?"

"Of course. I don't mind the glasses. I like that you can see," he teased.

"Loyal, it's just, if you're looking for someone to, uh, court, I don't think we'd suit."

She caught him off guard. Though he had been picking her up, spending time with her, and meeting her in the morning, he hadn't actually thought of those things as courting gestures. Though, of course they were.

He was merely a man, but even he knew such advances were signs of interest. "Do we have to think about the future? I just like being with you. Isn't that enough for now?"

She looked at him with consideration. "Perhaps it is."

"And, Ella, there's not a thing wrong with you. I can promise you that. Any man would be grateful for your companionship."

"You almost sound as if you mean that."

"I do. Now have a donut." He reached into the sack and pulled out a cinnamon twist.

Her eyes lit up. "That's my favorite."

"I know." While she took her first bite, he said, "Who's been telling you such things, anyway?"

"No one special. Just a friend."

"Dorothy?"

"Jah," she allowed after she swallowed. "Things with her haven't gotten much better. The other night, when we were at the farm, she came into my place uninvited. She left a note on the counter." She paused, then added, "And I know she opened some of my drawers and cabinets."

"That's not good."

Biting her lip again, Ella said, "She told me again not to see you. Matter of fact, she didn't like me seeing Corinne, either."

"Oh, Ella."

"I'm afraid I don't know what to do."

"How about I talk to her?"

"And what would you say, Loyal?"

"I'd say who you are friends with is none of her concern."

"I agree, but it might only make things worse." She jumped to her feet. "I need to go to work, Loyal."

"I'll walk you there."

"Dorothy's working. Would you mind much if you didn't?"

"Now you don't even want her to see us together?" Loyal was pretty sure he was never going to understand a woman's mind. "Ella, her interest makes no sense."

"I know that. But if she sees us together, she'll do nothing but want to talk about her opinions all day. And that makes for a terribly long day." She edged away. "I thank you for the donut. And your time, and your ears. Seeing you, and talking things over with you, helped me much. It was a mighty *gut* treat, Loyal."

"I'll see you soon," he promised. "Good-bye."

He was tempted to add something else, something about how he wanted to take her to the farm again, but she'd already turned and was walking at a quick pace toward the city square.

And though he had a lot to do, he decided that perhaps it was time to learn a little bit more about Dorothy Zook.

Mary Zehr finally came back into John's shop just a little after ten. It was the first time she'd ever arrived without Abel, and John thought she looked even younger without a growing boy dwarfing her slim frame.

"Hi," he said. "I was wondering if you were ever going to stop by again."

"Oh? Well, a person can't eat donuts too much, you know."

She seemed vaguely hesitant. Not quite looking at him in the eye. John wondered what was wrong.

Hoping to encourage her to talk a bit, to let him into her life, he smiled. "So, not even Abel can eat donuts all day, hmm?"

But instead of smiling right back at him, tears welled up in her eyes.

John darted around the counter and reached for her hand. "Hey, what's wrong?"

For a split second, Mary's hand relaxed in his, then she pulled it away and straightened. "It's nothing. Just that I'm not quite sure what to do with him."

He guided her to a table near the back wall, where few people ever sat, giving her at least a modicum of privacy. After she sat, he pulled out a chair next to her. "What's going on? Is he pulling away?"

She nodded. "For a long time, it's just

been him and me against the world. But now"—her lip trembled—"now, I'm afraid, it's just me."

Struggling to keep his expression open and his voice soft, he said, "If I told you it was his age, would you believe me?"

"Nee."

She was certainly honest! He couldn't help but laugh. "Oh, Mary. I'm no parent, but I remember getting letters from my brother Jacob about his three boys. They all pull away, I think. I know I did."

"Truly?"

"Definitely. It's part of growing up."

With a sniff, she looked at him doubtfully. "Then what happens?"

"Then they come back." Even as he said the words, he couldn't help but reflect that there was more than a little bit of irony there. After all, he was living proof that people came back—sometimes even after twenty years.

"I don't know what to do in the meantime." She traced a circle on the table with one neatly trimmed nail. "He got mad at me this morning when I tried to help him make his lunch for school." Raising her chin, she shook her head. "I know it doesn't sound like that's terribly important, but it still makes me sad."

"I'm sure it does." He was prevented from continuing when the door opened. "Will you stay here for a moment? I'll help these folks, then bring us some coffee and donuts."

As if aware that they were seated by themselves, Mary braced her hands on the table like she was ready to pop up. "John, maybe—"

"Please? Please stay?"

Almost reluctantly, she nodded.

Smiling at the group of four teenagers that came in, he got their donuts, poured two full mugs of hot coffee, and prepared one latte.

Then he set another pot to brewing, put the last cinnamon roll on a plate for Mary, and brought back two cups of coffee and her treat. "Here we go."

Right away, she cut off a corner of the bun and popped it into her mouth. A momentary look of bliss transformed her face, making him realize that Mary had a sweet tooth.

And something else. This wasn't just friendly concern or pity for her plight he was feeling.

Nope, he was attracted to both her angelic looks and her sweet, caring nature. Once more, he was becoming attracted to the way she made him feel . . . like he was valued.

However, he instinctively knew she would shy away from any romantic gestures he made. So it was best to keep things easy. With that in mind, he did his best to concentrate on Abel. "Mary, what I think you need is some help."

"I have help—"

"I mean for Abel. Boys need a male influence. You know, someone to cut up with."

Her eyes widened. "I don't know what that means."

"Nothing bad," he promised with a smile. "I'm just trying to say that it's been my experience that boys need someone to be boys with. To do all those things moms get mad at them for."

"Like play basketball?"

"Something like that." Actually, John had been thinking more of something along the lines of a little baser behavior. To talk about things that moms didn't want to think about. To burp and make bad jokes and

say things that weren't entirely appropriate. Nothing too bad.

She tugged in the bottom of her lip
again, obviously trying hard to think of
someone who could be that person for her
boy.

"Do you have someone in your life who
could be there for Abel?" he asked.

She stared hard at him. "I think so," she
said slowly.

He relaxed. "Oh, good. Who?"

"You," she said just as she took another
bite of that cinnamon bun and once again
closed her eyes with happiness.

His mouth went dry, but whether it was
from her pronouncement or that look on
her face, he wasn't sure.

"Mary, I don't know if that's a good idea."

Her eyes popped open. "Why?"

"Well, I'm not Amish . . ."

"I know. But you were. At least, you grew
up in an Amish home, yes?"

"Yes—"

"And I don't need help with Abel to be
Amish. I know how to teach him to value
our faith and way of life," she said with a
small smile.

Mary was sitting there teasing him?

John's stomach sank. Second by second, things were turning out of control.

She brightened. "I know! Perhaps my Abel could work here with you for a bit? They don't have much work for him at the hardware store."

"I don't have a lot of work here . . ."

"But that's *gut,* yes? Then you two would have lots of time to talk and visit." A line formed between her brows. "And you could do all those 'boy' things you were alluding to."

More customers came in, and then more after that. Just like the Lord was teasing him. Showing him that he had quite a busy shop in spite of what he told Mary.

John stood up. "I need to get to work."

"I'm sure you do. You're a terribly busy man." She speared another piece of pastry with her fork. "But, John, will you consider this?"

"Sure. Of course," he said as she took another bite. "Um. Come by tomorrow with Abel and we'll talk. Okay?"

"All right," she said with a smile. "And, John?"

"Yes?"

"Danke."

"You're very welcome," he said. He smiled wanly, before walking behind the counter. But in that brief amount of time, he said a quick word to the Lord.

I hear you, Lord. I hear you loud and clear, he said silently. After days and weeks of waiting for a sign from Him, the Lord had brought Mary to his door and the perfect reason for the two of them to spend more time together.

Now it was time to listen.

Chapter 17

Near the end of the workday, Ella discovered Dorothy shelving books in the children's section. For a moment, she watched her. As usual, Dorothy was a silent worker, merely shelving the books and organizing stacks with little more than a distracted glance at any of the patrons. Because of her sour expression, most of the children gave Dorothy wide berth.

Ella was tempted to avoid Dorothy as well, but she knew she couldn't behave so childishly. The plain and simple truth was that she couldn't avoid Dorothy forever.

And, well, not trusting Dorothy's recent moods, Ella figured it would be safer to speak with her in a public place.

Picking up a stack of books left on a table, Ella straightened her shoulders and approached her.

"Dorothy, here you are. All day I've been trying to have a word with you."

For the briefest of seconds, Dorothy froze. Then she visibly gathered her composure, placing her palms on a stretch of bare shelf as if to stabilize herself. Finally, she spoke. "I've been here all along. What did you need help with?"

Irritation sliced through Ella as she realized that, once again, Dorothy was going to place all responsibility—and fault—with her. "It's not that. I wanted to speak to you about the note you left me last night."

Still keeping her hands on the shelf, Dorothy stared straight ahead. "Oh. I wondered when you were going to thank me for the meal."

Ella was stunned. This was the exact opposite of the reaction that she'd been expecting. She'd been expecting anger and accusations. Or even a denial. Definitely not such a chiding remark. "Dorothy," she sputtered, "you were in my home. Without my permission."

"No, that is not true." Turning her head, Dorothy finally pinned Ella with a penetrating gaze. "It's *mei haus*."

"I know it's your house, but I am renting from you. That counts as ownership, I think."

Dorothy turned away and rolled her cart of books two feet away. For a moment, Ella watched her actions in surprise.

The more closely she worked with Dorothy, the more evident it was that this woman thought of no one else's needs but her own.

While it was true she didn't have a wealth of skills when it came to working and socializing with others, even Ella knew she'd never been this rude to anyone in her life! Becoming increasingly frustrated, she followed her friend down another cramped aisle and continued her objections. "Dorothy, I don't want you entering my home when I'm not there. It makes me uncomfortable."

Silence between them lingered. Dorothy pulled a book from the cart, bent down on one knee, and slid it into the correct spot. When she got to her feet, she finally gave Ella her attention. "You are making me uncomfortable, too," she said. "You are not acting like I'd hoped you would. None of this is like how things were supposed to be."

"How did you imagine things would be?"

"I had thought you would want me in your life." Her voice hardening, Dorothy added, "Ella, we were supposed to do things together."

"Dorothy, we have."

"Barely. I had planned for us to work together and eat our meals together, too. I thought we were going to be best friends. Best friends who would push aside duties for each other."

Ella stared at her in confusion. "What duties are you talking about?"

"About your obligations to that man, of course."

"My wanting to be with Loyal is most certainly not an obligation."

"If he's not a duty, then it's even worse. Instead of returning the friendship I've offered, you are taking me for granted."

"I've done no such thing—"

Dorothy's voice rose as she stepped forward, crowding Ella. "How else can you explain the way you've been leaving me to be with him? It's made me sick every time you've left me to see that man."

"That man's name is Loyal."

"You shouldn't be even talking with him, let alone spending so much time in his company."

"Dorothy, he's my friend."

"He bought your farm. He bought your life."

That's where Dorothy was wrong. He'd bought her farm, but not what really counted. He bought things that had been important to her, but now she was realizing that those things had been just that— merely items that meant little. He hadn't bought what was in her heart. Or anything that made her who she was.

Instead, he'd shown her many ways that he'd valued those things.

"He's not my enemy," she tried to explain. "All he did was buy my family's farm. And I was grateful for that. I'd put it up for auction."

"He pushed you out of your house. And now he's driving us farther apart."

"Dorothy, I'm afraid you have things all wrong." When a parent glanced their way with concern, Ella knew their discussion would have to end. What she'd hoped would be a simple matter of clarifying their boundaries was becoming something else entirely different. "Perhaps we could talk on the way home tonight."

"You'll have time?" Pure hurt burned deep in her eyes. "You're not going out with *him* again?"

"No."

"All right, then. I will see you for supper."

As Ella turned around, she felt her spirits fall. For too long, she'd gone to bed each night with a prayer to God, asking Him to give her a future that was more vibrant and filled with hope than the previous year had been.

And it seemed like He was doing that. He had given her a wonderful job and children like Katie to get to know. And new friendships like the one she was having with Loyal.

But why had he also given her such a confusing relationship with Dorothy? She'd been the one person Ella was sure she would be comfortable with.

But instead of comfort, she was finding only frustration and unease.

And the niggling sense that things were about to get worse.

Chapter 18

"You didn't have to come with me to the doctor, you know," Mattie told Lucy as they rode in the back of Charlie's van to the Geauga County Medical Center.

"Sure I did. I promised you I'd be with you every step of the way."

Remembering how Lucy had come by train to help take care of her for a whole month while she'd been receiving chemotherapy treatments, Mattie knew that her friend had more than fulfilled her promise. "Hopefully, this journey will be over one day."

Lucy paused as she narrowed her eyes. "What's going on?"

"Nothing."

"I know you, Mattie, and I know that tone in your voice. I know you almost better than I know myself. What's happened?"

"I . . . I found another lump," she reluctantly admitted. "It's under my arm."

Lucy's eyes widened and she breathed in sharply. "When?"

"A few days ago."

"Is that why you're going in today? The doctor wanted to see you right away?"

"No, this is simply a checkup."

"He's not worried? What did he say? Is this normal?" The questions came out in a rush. Forceful.

So forceful that Mattie had to smile in spite of the million butterflies fluttering in her stomach. "What happened to my shy, timid friend Lucy?"

After a moment's pause, Lucy grinned, too. "She's inside of me still. But now I let this bossy part speak sometimes, too. Forgive me, am I making you uncomfortable?"

"*Verra* much so." She cleared her throat. "So will you stop the questions now?"

"*Nee.* Mattie, what did the *doktah* say?"

"I haven't told anyone."

Lucy blinked. "No one?"

"Well, you," Mattie allowed.

"Are you going to tell the *doktah* today?"

"I wasn't going to, but I guess I should." Looking at Lucy's determined expression, Mattie said, "After all, I have a feeling if I don't say anything, you will. Right?"

"Oh, yes."

Mattie watched Charlie exit the highway and turn right. In the distance, she could already see the medical center looming. And though the men and women who worked there had been kind to her, she still felt a bit of distaste when she eyed the place.

She so did not want to go back to twice-weekly visits. To sitting in a chair hooked up to too many needles.

"I don't want to go through this again," she finally whispered. "I don't think I can survive another round of chemotherapy."

"Let's not jump to conclusions." Lucy slipped her hand through hers and squeezed tightly. "But if that's what is needed, why . . . yes, you can. You can do anything you want, with God's help."

"But I don't want this."

"Then let me rephrase my words. You can survive just about anything, with God's help."

Mattie swallowed hard. Lucy had been through so much, she knew her friend believed that with all her heart.

It wasn't the same for Mattie. Over the last year, her faith had steadily dissipated, like air out of a balloon. Now there was hardly any faith left.

Though she'd talked to Lucy about it, Lucy was under the impression that Mattie had worked through her issues and was a believer again. But that certainly wasn't the truth.

Of course, that was another secret she'd been holding on to.

That one, at least, she'd been able to keep to herself.

"What do you know about Dorothy Zook, Mamm?" Loyal asked when they were driving to the Middlefield Wal-Mart, his mother's all-time favorite place to shop.

"Dorothy?" she asked in surprise. "Not too much. Why?"

"She's Ella Hostetler's new landlady," he said, hoping he sounded more casual and nonchalant than he felt. "They seem to be good friends."

"And?"

He jangled Beauty's reins as the light turned and they continued down the road. "And I don't know too much about Dorothy."

She paused a second, obviously waiting for a better answer than the one he gave. "Well, truthfully, I don't know too much about her, either," she finally murmured. "As you know, Dorothy's about ten years older than all of you. Because of the age difference, you all never played together . . ."

Privately, Loyal wondered if he or Calvin or Graham would've been her playmates even if they had seen each other every day. He rather doubted it.

After another moment's reflection, his *mamm* added, "Did you know she's from a big family? She's one of eight children."

That did surprise him. "I've only seen her alone. Where is the rest of her family?"

"They moved away when she was fourteen or fifteen. I think they moved to Indiana. Or maybe even Canada?" she pondered, staring out at the trees and flowering bushes they passed. "Someplace far."

"Why didn't Dorothy go with them? Surely she was too young to stay by herself."

"From what I understand, she had plans here and refused to leave."

"And her parents let her?"

"I suppose so. She stayed with Lydia Schrock." She darted a glance his way. "Do you remember her? She was kind of a crusty old woman. Dorothy moved to her house and became something of her caretaker."

What teenage girl would take care of a grumpy elderly lady by choice? "Why on earth would she do that?"

"Well, this is only hearsay . . . but I heard she stayed for a boy."

"What happened with that?"

"A few months after her family moved and she started working for Mrs. Schrock, the boy broke up with her."

"Ouch."

Looking uncomfortable, his mother nodded. "I think there were some mighty bad things said."

Against his will, Loyal felt sorry for Dorothy. "So, then, what did she do?"

"She stayed here and continued working."

"Why didn't she just go to her family?"

"I'm not sure . . ."

Glancing to his right, he smiled. He knew that look on his mother's face. It was slightly guilt-ridden—the same expression she wore when she ate two desserts or slept in.

She was feeling bad for talking about Dorothy's history.

But though he knew gossiping was a sin, he felt justified in pushing just a little bit more. After all, he really was concerned about Ella's friendship with Dorothy.

"Mamm, we've gossiped this much, you might as well tell me the whole story."

"All right. Well, I heard that she did write to them, but that Mrs. Schrock had written to them, too. And while Dorothy said she wanted to leave Jacob's Crossing and start over, Lydia didn't paint quite as good a picture. She either said she couldn't live without Dorothy, or made it sound like Dorothy had been acting foolishly with that boy. No matter what, the family gently told her to stay put, at least for a bit."

"She never joined her family, did she?"

His mom shook her head with regret. "No, she didn't. About a year after all this took place, old Lydia died. She left some money for Dorothy. Dorothy used it for the house she's living in, and then she went to work at the library."

"It's a pretty sad story, Mamm. That poor girl was used by a man, used by Lydia, and then abandoned by her family."

"It is sad. Terribly sad. No one ever speaks of it."

"If people did, maybe she wouldn't be so strange," he muttered, as he entered the Wal-Mart parking lot and veered left toward the buggy area. "I guess she never got back with that boy?"

"She did not. He married, then moved to Sugarcreek or Berlin or somewhere." As Loyal parked the buggy in the covered area and they exited the buggy, his mom looked at him curiously. "It's your turn now. How interested in Ella are you?"

"I'm not sure . . ."

"Loyal."

"All right. I know I'm far more interested in her than I thought I would ever be. I like her, Mamm. She's got a good spirit," he added as they walked to the entrance of the supercenter. "But, Mamm, this Dorothy doesn't seem to have her best interests at heart."

"Has Ella told you this?"

"Yes. Well, to some extent she has. Ella's been through a lot. She's now doing the kinds of things she's always wanted to do. She's working and making new friends."

"Wasn't the library Dorothy's doing?"

"Yes, but I'm starting to think that the library job and her house was all so Dorothy could keep track of Ella. That's wrong, don't you think?"

Her mouth pursed. "If that's what happening . . . then, yes, it is disturbing."

Loyal nodded.

Grasping his arm, his mother leaned closer. "But, Loyal, Son. Don't forget something."

He paused. "What?"

"It's been my experience that people don't care to have you interfere in their lives without good reason," she warned. "If you do try to break their friendship, both women will be hurt—and Ella might never forgive you."

Though his mother's words caused a chill to run through him, he couldn't escape the belief that he was the one in the right. His motives were justified. "I'd only be protecting her. For her own good."

"She will only be appreciative of it if she sees things your way," she said slowly. "If she doesn't, you could be causing nothing but pain."

Loyal stood still while his mother stepped forward and took a shopping cart.

As she started wheeling it into the cool, air-conditioned building, she looked at him again. "And, Loyal Weaver, I think all of us would agree that Dorothy has been through enough pain already."

It irked him, but Loyal nodded. Once again, his mother was right. It seemed, no matter what, she was always right.

Chapter 19

No one seemed to understand how hard it was to be Katie Weaver. No one. Except maybe Miss Ella.

Though she had three big brothers and a mother who seemed to see and know everything, Katie sometimes felt like she was always being shuffled around.

It truly was difficult to be very small when everyone else in the family was so terribly big. And old!

Today was the perfect example. With all three of her brothers needing to be in the fields and her mother already having promised to can all day, Katie had been told to stay with Lucy.

Well, actually, Mamm had told her to either stay with Lucy or sit in the hot kitchen and watch all the ladies can carrots and beans.

Then, just as Katie had settled in by Lucy's side at the library, even Lucy had found something else to do than be with her.

Next thing Katie knew, she was being handed over to Miss Ella. And though Miss Ella really was her favorite librarian, Katie still wasn't too happy about it.

"Katie, I'm so glad you are going to walk home with me today," Miss Ella said with a kind smile. "I feel so lucky your family is letting you keep me company this afternoon."

Though it was on the tip of Katie's tongue to tell Miss Ella that she got it all wrong—that her family wasn't being kind, they just didn't have time to go get her—she decided to keep quiet.

"Can we bring some books back to your home?"

"Perhaps. How many do you want to check out today?"

"Four."

"Four is just fine," Ella said agreeably.

"I mean, maybe five," she sputtered. Unable to stand still, Katie twisted her fingers. "How about five?"

Miss Ella's lips twitched. "We could probably check out five."

"Or six?" she blurted, unable to help herself. She loved getting picture books from the library. She loved carefully writing the titles down on the paper.

And she really loved when Miss Ella put special gold stars on her reading form. They were so shiny and sparkly.

"Six?" Ella's eyebrows rose over the gold rims of her glasses. For one second, Katie was sure Miss Ella's eyes lit up before she turned almost stern. "I think not."

"But—"

"It is never a good thing to be greedy, Katie. Don't you forget that. Plus, there needs to be some *bichah* left for other *kinner.*"

Katie supposed Ella was right. There did need to be plenty of books left for other children. "I won't forget."

"All right, then. I'll wait here while you pick out your books."

"It won't take me long. I already know which ones I want."

Miss Ella's lips twitched. "Take your time, Katie. When you get your books, I'll check them out."

Katie rushed over to the children's section. Though she was tempted to look at some of the new books by the bean-bag chairs, she pulled the ones she'd hoped to have and handed them to Miss Ella.

With little fuss, Miss Ella scanned the books through a machine and put little cards in the book pockets. "Let's go now, yes?" Ella reached down and held out a hand. Katie lifted her palm and clung to Ella's hand happily. After saying goodbye to Ms. Donovan, they walked down the library's steps and headed to the left.

Holding Miss Ella's hand, everything looked brighter and prettier. The patch of fall pansies were more purple, the bed of begonias looked as red as the brick on the courthouse.

Katie began to skip, swinging Miss Ella's arm as they walked down the sidewalk. She had to skid to a stop when an *Englischer* walked by with his Dalmatian; and then a group of English teenagers approached, all of them punching buttons on their phones and laughing.

When one teenager smiled at her, Katie smiled right back.

"Do you like living in town, Miss Ella?" she asked when they started walking again.

"Today I do."

"Why today?"

Miss Ella smiled. "Because it means I get to do two special things."

"What?"

"I get to have a visitor, and it gives me an excuse to stop at the Kaffi Haus."

Katie wrinkled her nose. "I don't like coffee."

"I didn't imagine you would," Miss Ella replied, obviously trying to hide a smile as she held out her hand. "But perhaps you would like a donut? They have all kinds there."

"You're going to buy us some?"

Ella nodded. "Of course."

Katie slipped her hand back into Ella's. "Then I can't wait. I'm hungry." As soon as she blurted that, she winced. If her mother had been there, she would have scolded her, for sure.

But Ella didn't look mad at all. She just laughed. "I'm *hungerich, too.*"

A warm burst of happiness floated through Katie. Some of the kids she knew were a little afraid of Ella. Ella was very tall. Almost as tall as the men. And her glasses made her eyes look too big.

But Katie thought she was one of the nicest people in the world. She read all the good stories, and she had a merry laugh that seemed to make her whole body wiggle.

Remembering how Miss Ella had stared at Loyal when he wasn't looking, Katie began to plan. If Miss Ella was a part of their family, then Katie would never run out of books, because surely Ella wouldn't put a limit on the numbers of books family members could check out.

If Miss Ella married Loyal, then Katie could go get donuts all the time. And she'd have someone to laugh with, too.

"I like being with you, Miss Ella," she blurted.

Ella laughed merrily again, making crinkly lines around her eyes. "And, I, Miss Katie, like being with you."

*   *   *

It had been a good day, Ella decided as she walked Katie up the front steps of her apartment. Ms. Donovan had complimented her work ethic that morning, and then, of course, there had been Lucy's visit, with Katie in tow.

"Feel free to tell me no, Ella," Lucy had said. "But is there any way I could leave Katie here with you for three hours? Mattie has a doctor's appointment today and everyone else has other commitments."

Ella hadn't waited even a half-second to accept. "I don't mind at all, though I get off at three o'clock today."

Lucy's eyes widened. "Oh! I couldn't ask you to stay longer. Don't worry, I'll just take her with me."

But Ella could only imagine how things would be at the medical center with Katie in tow. "What I meant to say was that I would be happy to take her home with me."

"I couldn't ask you to do that . . ."

"Whyever not? I'm happy to offer."

After glancing Katie's way, Lucy finally nodded. "*Danke*. Let me go speak with Katie, then I'll be on my way."

"Lucy, is everything all right with Mattie?"

She bit her lip. "I hope so." Moments

later, after a quick hug and visit with Katie, she'd darted off.

After getting Katie's books, they'd walked down the street, got a snack for Katie, and visited with John Weaver. Then, after another three blocks' walk, they arrived at her home.

As Ella unlocked the door, she handed Katie the book bag she'd been carrying. "It's now your turn to hold this," she teased. "All of your books almost made my shoulder ache."

Katie's eyes widened with worry, then when she saw that Ella was teasing, crinkled with glee. "Miss Ella, you're funny!" she said.

As soon as the door opened, she wrinkled her nose. "But your house smells yucky."

Stepping in, Ella had to agree. The air smelled thick and stale . . . like rotten food?

But how could that be?

Feeling thoroughly confused, Ella leaned down and stared hard at her tiny guest. "Katie, you stay by the door and keep it open for me, would you? I'm going to go in and open some windows."

"I'll hold it *way* open."

As Ella stepped inside, her heart started beating quicker, right in sync with her spirits sinking lower. Once again, it was obvious that someone else had been in her apartment. Her knitting basket was on its side, the needles and yarn strewn in a knotted mess across the floor.

The book that she'd checked out of the new release section of the library had been ripped in half!

Tears burned her eyes. Now she was not only going to have to pay for it, but would have to tell Jayne that she'd somehow damaged a brand-new book.

But when she took two steps farther into the kitchen, she saw the reason for the smell: the chicken dinner that Dorothy had made a week ago was sitting on the counter. Spoiled.

Two flies buzzed above the rotten chicken, sticky noodles, and wilted salad.

Ella pressed a hand to her mouth as she attempted to retrace what had happened. With a weary heart, she remembered taking a bite of Dorothy's dinner, but not enjoying the flavors at all. It had been too salty, and all a bit rubbery in texture. In addition, Ella had worried that maybe the chicken hadn't been all that fresh.

Worried about possibly getting sick—and definitely knowing that the meal would not be enjoyed—she'd thrown it in the trash.

But now, here it was, sitting on her kitchen counter on one of her plates—after sitting in a garbage can outside for two days!

Obviously, only one person could have done such a thing. No, Ella corrected herself. Only one person had done such a thing: Dorothy.

Pain, sharp and biting, rushed through Ella with as much force as a knife blade. She'd always praised the Lord for Dorothy's friendship. She'd been so thankful when Dorothy had offered her this place to live, at such a reasonable price, too.

But now nothing was clear. Surely there could be no reason for Dorothy's actions except for pure hatred and spite.

But what was even the correct way to respond? Ella wished she knew more about English laws. Wasn't it against the law for Dorothy to do what she was doing?

Was this something that she should contact the police about? But what if they laughed at her?

And how would she even know where to contact them? She had no idea where the police station was.

"Miss Ella, are ya goin' to open a window?"

"Oh, *jah*!" Quickly, she rushed to the window over the sink and pushed it up.

"Did you figure out the smell?" Katie called from the door, bringing her back to the present. "And can I move yet?"

What Ella wanted to do was curl up in a ball and cry. This violation of her privacy was terribly upsetting. For Dorothy to ruin a book and put that dinner on her counter, too—well, it was bordering on very scary.

But in the forefront of her mind was her obligation to Katie. She'd promised Lucy that she would look after the little girl. And that promise needed to be kept, no matter what the circumstances.

So for now, she'd put on a happier face and move on. And decide later what she was going to do about Dorothy.

"Um. Of course, child. Come here. Come help me use this kitchen chair to prop open the door. Perhaps the breeze will air out the room."

After they did that, Katie looked at her

with wide eyes. "Are you all right, Miss Ella? You look like you're about to cry."

"That's because I am," she admitted. "But I will be fine. Don't worry none."

Katie touched her arm. "Miss Ella? Are you mad at me? Are you sorry that I'm with ya? Because I talk too much?"

The little girl looked so worried—her blue eyes so wide-eyed and frantic—Ella immediately got down on one knee and enfolded her in a hug. "Not at all, child. As a matter of fact, I'm terribly glad you are here. I need a friend right now."

Instantly Katie's arms flung around her middle and hung on tight. "No one's ever said they needed me before," Katie whispered.

"Well, I certainly do. Katie Weaver, your hug is exactly what I needed, right this minute. You'll never know how very happy I am to have you with me right now."

With that, the little girl flung her arms around her once again. Unable to hold back her emotions any longer, Ella bent her head and wept.

Chapter 20

After working side by side with Abel for three hours, John came to the conclusion that it wasn't masculine roughhousing or cutting up that the boy wanted.

It was just someone to talk to.

During their time together, the boy talked to John about his best friend and the girl he kind of liked, but wasn't sure if she liked him back.

John heard about Abel's favorite food—tacos; and the dinner his mother was inordinately fond of cooking—chicken casserole.

Through all the conversations, Abel washed down tables and swept the floor, taking directions easily, and doing his best.

Remembering how surly he used be while doing chores, John was very impressed with the boy.

About an hour before he was supposed to leave, John figured it would be a good idea to talk to Abel about things that were a little more serious. After all, John had a very good feeling that Mary was going to be asking him questions.

"Abel, how about a soda?"

"Do you have root beer?"

"I do. Want one of those?" When the boy nodded, John popped the tops off two glass bottles, then sat down across from him at the table. "You did a good job today. I appreciate it."

"Thanks."

"Do you think this job is going to work out for you? If it doesn't, you can let me know . . ."

"No, I like it," Abel answered quickly.

"I like having you here." John wondered how to skim around things, but there didn't seem to be a real easy way to do it. So, he just dived right in. "I'm getting the feeling your mom is a little worried about you."

Abel paused as a new wariness entered his eyes. "She tell you that?"

"Not in so many words. Is there something bothering you?"

"Not really." But something darker flashed into the boy's eyes.

"If you ever do feel like talking, I keep pretty good secrets."

Abel shook his head. "It's nothing like that. I just miss having a *daed* sometimes. It's awfully quiet at my *haus*."

"'Cause it's just you and your mom?"

Abel nodded. "People say she should have married again."

John tamped down the twinge of jealousy that rose inside of him. He had no right to be feeling possessive about Mary. But still, the idea of her keeping company with another man was difficult to swallow. "Is there someone special that she is interested in?" he asked lightly. Hoping that he sounded more nonchalant than he felt.

"Nee," Abel said quickly. "My *daed*, I hardly remember him, but he liked to laugh. Some of the men who like my mother are too serious. They're always frowning."

"That would be hard."

Abel nodded. "But she needs to find

someone pretty soon. I'm growing up, you know?"

Ah. Maybe they were finally getting to the heart of the matter. "Are you worried about your *mamm*? Worried about her being alone?"

"Kind of." He paused to sip his root beer. "She would be sad to be alone the rest of her life."

John suspected she would be. After all, he had certainly been lonely over the years. "You're pretty mature, Abel. Lots of boys wouldn't be thinking about their moms like that."

He shrugged. "She's my *mamm*."

John couldn't help but smile as he stood up. "That says it all, Abel." After glancing at his watch, he said, "Speaking of your mother, she's going to be looking for you if you don't get on your way. I'll see you next week."

"Can I take the rest of my root beer?"

"Of course," he said softly. As Abel left, John realized that the tables had certainly turned on that conversation. Here, he'd hoped to give Abel sage advice, but instead, it was the boy who'd taught him a thing or two.

No one wanted to be alone forever. And

after almost twenty years, John knew it was past time to stop being afraid of relationships and to move forward.

Ella's front door was wide open when Loyal arrived at her doorstep a little after six in the evening.

Beside him, Graham paused on the stairs. "Does she usually keep her doors open like this?"

"I don't know. I haven't been here all that much."

"Ah." Graham's tone was speculative, but there was a twinkle in his eyes that told Loyal he was holding a few thoughts to himself.

Which made Loyal irritated. "Ella and I are merely friends."

"So you've told me. Many times."

As Loyal felt his cheeks heat, he wondered how else he could explain his relationship when Ella appeared at the door. "Hi," he said, sounding awkward even to his ears.

Her answering smile could only be described as shaky. "Loyal and Graham, hello. I didn't know you both were going to pick up Katie."

"Katie's such a handful, I thought Loyal might need a hand," Graham said.

"I am not a handful," Katie announced, joining them on the front porch. "I've been helpful today, haven't I, Miss Ella?"

"Indeed you have."

Loyal watched Ella's hand shake as she placed it on his little sister's shoulder. Something wasn't quite right. "Ella, why do you have your door open?"

"Someone put bad food in here," Katie said in a rush. "And that person ripped pages out of Ella's book. And then ripped them in half!"

Beside him, Graham stiffened. Loyal stepped inside. The room looked fine. He sniffed the air. It did smell a little sour, but nothing too horrible. Turning around, he faced Ella who was still standing at the door, half looking like she didn't want to even enter her own home. "Ella, what happened?"

A tear escaped her eye and traipsed down her cheek. Warily, she glanced Graham's way.

"He can be trusted," Loyal said quietly. "I can promise you that."

After taking a deep breath, Ella spoke.

"When Katie and I came home, it was obvious someone had been in here without my permission. Pages were ripped out of my book, and there was a dinner on a plate . . ." Her voice hitched and another tear escaped as she visibly tried to regain control of herself.

"Take your time," Loyal murmured, his heart aching for her.

But his sister, of course, was not near as patient. "It was a really awful dinner. It smelled!"

Ella winced.

"Katie, hush," Graham ordered.

Loyal closed the distance between them and took her hand. Immediately, her fingers closed around his. "Your hand is like ice," he said. "You need to sit down."

She looked around with a wary eye. "I know. I'm still half afraid of what else I'll find."

"I'll sit with you." Once he had her settled, their knees touching and her hand still clasped in between his own, Loyal spoke again. "Tell me about the dinner."

"A few days ago, Dorothy had made me a dinner, but I never ate it. Because it was the evening we had the picnic."

"I remember."

"She had let herself in and put it in my refrigerator. Without me knowing," she added haltingly. Pulling her hand from his, she clasped her hands together tightly.

"She shouldn't be coming in here without your permission," Graham said as he sat in a single chair across from them.

"That's what I told Dorothy," Ella said. "But she corrected me. Saying that it's her home, and she was only doing me a favor." She shook her head, as if to clear it. "Anyway, the food didn't smell good to me, and the act behind it made me uncomfortable. So even though it was a waste, I threw the dinner out and put it in the garbage can outside. Today, when we walked in, I found the food. She'd taken it out of the trash and put it on a plate."

A shiver ran up Loyal's spine. "This is all very disturbing, Ella."

She bit her lip and nodded. "I cleaned things up and then sat with Katie, wondering what to do." Looking directly into his eyes, she said, "Loyal, I'm starting to feel afraid. I've never felt like this before in my life! Not even when I was home alone taking care of my mother who was *dying.*"

Graham rested his elbows on his knees. Quietly, he said, "I think you should go to the police."

"For such silly things?"

"Are they silly?" Graham countered. "Dorothy is entering your home without you knowing and going through your trash. In my opinion, this is verging on something darker than silliness."

As Loyal examined the lines of worry about Ella's eyes, a fierce protectiveness built. "I'm inclined to agree."

"Maybe she's merely sick," Ella murmured.

"What kind of sickness is that?"

"I'm just not eager to get outsiders involved."

Loyal knew Ella was struggling with a great many things—with Dorothy, her new living situation, and even grief about her mother. Any one of those things would be a difficult burden. But altogether, they would be overwhelming.

"How about you and I speak to the bishop? Perhaps he could pay a call to Dorothy?"

"Could that be done?"

"Certainly. And perhaps that would be

more meaningful to her. All of us want to be good stewards of our church and of our faith. The only way we can do that is by following our rules and standards."

She exhaled. "I would like to go that route. I trust the bishop."

"*Gut.* Then it's settled. I'll set up the meeting and then we'll go together."

She looked from Graham to Loyal. "What would I do without you two? Thank you for the advice and the comfort. I'm grateful."

When Ella treated him to a tremulous smile, he couldn't help but reach out to her and clasp her hand. Her fingers were still cold.

The only remedy was to wrap his other hand around hers. "Things will get better. I promise, they will," he said, hoping this was a promise he'd be able to keep.

An hour later, when they were almost home and Katie was sound asleep in the buggy, sprawled across Graham's lap, Graham spoke. "Are you ever going to talk to me about Ella?"

Loyal looked at him curiously. "It's pretty much all arranged. You know that. I'm going to speak with the bishop in the morning and take Ella by to discuss things. Hopefully in a matter of days, Ella will be able to live with some semblance of peace."

"Loyal . . . I'm talking about your relationship with her."

"Oh."

"Yes," Graham said with a hint of a smile in his voice, *" 'Oh.' "*

Gripping the reins more firmly, Loyal guided their buggy around a parked car on the side of the road before continuing forward on the shoulder of the street. "Nothing specific has been discussed."

"But something is brewing between the two of you."

Loyal couldn't deny that. He also couldn't refute the confusion he was feeling about their relationship. "I've known Ella for most of my life, Graham. Why am I only now thinking of her differently? Why do I now care so much about her? About her feelings, about her happiness?"

"Perhaps it's God's time," Graham said after a moment. "Maybe the two of you weren't meant to have a relationship until now."

Graham's words made sense. Loyal firmly believed that the Lord watched over them, and that everything happened in His time. But he was still having trouble grappling with his feelings. He'd always imagined he'd become involved with a different sort of woman. A woman who was from a family like his, who'd had much of the same interests.

Maybe that didn't matter. What mattered was what was in a person's heart. Still struggling to understand himself, he said, "Graham, do you think Ella and I are an odd match?"

"Why would you ask?"

"You know why. In many ways, we couldn't be more different. She's so quiet. I've never been that way. She's been alone, independent for most of her life. I've always been surrounded by family."

"A person can't help their circumstances."

"That is true."

"And people do say opposites attract."

"We are certainly opposite," Loyal agreed. But what he wasn't ready to share was that those opposites intrigued him. He was discovering that he didn't want to be in the company of someone who acted just like him. Or who had the same strengths. No, he was now coming to realize that he wanted someone who was a little more introspective. A little quieter.

Graham crossed his one foot over the opposite knee. "Yes, there's a time and place for everything," he said primly.

Loyal mentally rolled his eyes. Graham was now spouting platitudes and clichés like an old woman. "Just tell me what you think. Tell me what you would do if you were me."

"All right. Truthfully? I never would have imagined the two of you together. But when you're with Ella, she seems to glow. And all of a sudden, I don't just see her glasses and notice how tall she is. I suddenly notice the spark of amusement in her eyes. And the kindness she shows toward others. And the way the two of you get along so well."

"So you think Ella and me might be a *gut* match?"

"Perhaps. But it doesn't really matter what I think, Loyal. All that matters is what you think."

"I don't know . . ."

"Loyal, nothing needs to be decided now, does it? You and Ella have plenty of time to figure things out, don'tcha think?"

He looked at Graham in surprise. "You know, that's the first thing you've told me that makes any sense!"

"Hopefully it won't be the last," Graham said dryly.

Chapter 21

After Mattie and Lucy returned from the latest doctor's appointment, Mattie sat down with her mother and told her the news. Another surgery had been scheduled.

As she'd expected, her mother struggled with the doctor's recommendation. Now her mother was wringing her hands so hard, Mattie feared they were about to fall off. "Oh, Mattie. I just can't believe you've got to have another operation in two days. What are we going to do?"

Mattie struggled to keep her voice steady and her expression neutral. Inside, however, she was doing the exact opposite. The doctor's news had shaken her to the core.

"We are going to need to remove this cyst right away, Mattie," he'd said, his expression grim.

"But it's not cancerous, right?"

"I don't know."

She'd wanted to lash out at him. To tell him that after all the rounds of chemotherapy, she was supposed to be cancer free forever.

But instead of offering her any words of encouragement, he'd just looked at Lucy. "Trish will come in and schedule Mattie's appointment. Then she'll direct you to the lab. We're going to need more blood."

Mattie had sat there, fuming. Feeling completely ignored. Ineffectual. "But, *Doktah—*"

He turned to her with sympathy in his eyes. "I *am* sorry, Mattie," he murmured before leaving. "I will pray for you."

"Bayda?" she fairly yelped as he left the room.

Lucy pressed a hand to her arm. "You're speaking Pennsylvania Dutch, Mattie."

With some dismay, Mattie realized that she was. Which brought her into a deeper depression—usually, she always did her best to speak proper English with all the medical personnel. Speaking that way made her think she was on more even ground with them.

For her to slip into *Deutsch* meant she was really rattled.

And now it was all she could do to stay afloat as she tried her best to comfort her mother. "Mamm, we mustn't get too concerned, *jah*? We've been through worse."

After wiping her eyes, her mother straightened and attempted to smile. "Mattie, of course you're right. I'm sorry. I don't mean to burden you with my worries. Of course everything is going to be fine."

"I bet so, too," Mattie replied. "I bet this is just a precaution."

"Definitely." She clapped her hands. "We need only to keep busy and not dwell so. God didn't bring you this far for no good reason, ain't so?" She rubbed her hands on the skirt of her dark gray dress. "I know! I think we should make ice cream. Don't you? It's the only thing that will cool us off on such a hot day. What flavor shall we make?"

"Vanilla?" Mattie blurted.

"That's what I was thinking, exactly." Reaching out, she grasped Mattie's hand.

Her mother's hand was cold. Cold with fear, Mattie assumed. Exactly the way she felt, too.

Even so, they looked at each other and smiled before heading into the kitchen to begin their task.

Both pretending that neither was worried at all.

Bishop Howard stared so hard at Ella, she could practically feel his piercing gaze burn into her skin.

"These things you've told me are hard to believe," he said quietly.

Though her palms were sweating, she looked right back at him. "I know."

"But they are the truth," Loyal spoke up. "I've witnessed much of what Ella is telling you."

"Oh, I believe you, Ella. I'm just greatly disturbed."

Pure relief filled her as she looked at the man who'd done so much for her mother. He'd visited their house almost daily at the very end of her mother's life. For that, Ella would always be grateful. "I haven't known what to do. Dorothy has been a good friend to me. But these things she's done . . ."

Her voice drifted off as she tried to find the words, the right words to convey her sense of worry and loss. "These things she's done have begun to make me feel afraid," she finally said. "Last night I could hardly close my eyes. I don't feel safe. I don't want to hurt Dorothy, but I also am starting not to trust her." Finally, she added, "Quite simply, I'm at a loss of what to do now."

"I'm glad you came to speak with me. I'll pray on this and then will visit with her."

"See, Ella, you are not alone," Loyal said, his voice full of encouragement. "Together, we will all help you. I promise."

After a few more minutes of conversation, Ella left the bishop with Loyal at her side. Though the day was warm, Ella was glad to stretch her legs. And for the time to visit with Loyal. Earlier, they'd also walked together, from Loyal's farm to the bishop's home.

"Do you feel a little better?" he asked.

Glancing his way, she found comfort in the honest look of concern in his eyes.

Suddenly, she realized that she wasn't alone, carrying these worries.

Loyal—along with God—was right there with her and wasn't going to give up on her, either. "I do," she said softly. "Though nothing's been decided, I was grateful to share my burdens."

"Don't make it a one-time thing, Ella. My shoulders are broad enough to carry your worries."

As Ella thought about how much he'd gone out of his way for her over the last few weeks, she glanced his way again. "Loyal, I want you to know . . . that I truly feel grateful to you. Over and over, you have done so much for me. And you didn't have to do any of it." Privately, she wondered why he had. After all, she had nothing to give him in return.

"I haven't done all that much. Just encouraged you to talk to some people."

"I wouldn't have spoken with the bishop if not for you."

"Maybe not today, but eventually you would have."

"You sound so certain. Why?"

"There's a strength in you, Ella. A

strength that shows you are used to being independent. You are a formidable woman."

He was smiling, and before she knew it, she was smiling, too . . . at the image. She, Ella Hostetler, a formidable woman? How could that be?

Usually she was always the one person who tried to blend in with the wall, not assert her will. "I'll take your words as a compliment."

"You should! You are a remarkable woman. And helpful, too."

"How so?"

"Well, you've helped us with Katie."

"Katie? That was no trouble. Katie is a dear. Such a joy."

"Such a handful," he corrected with a laugh. "We love her very much, but she has her moments that try my patience."

"As do we all."

Loyal blinked. "You're right. My brothers and I like to tease about Katie, but above all, we are always grateful for her."

"Oh, I know that. As for Katie, I have a feeling that she just wants some attention," she murmured, thinking for a moment of her own childhood. She'd loved her family dearly and had never minded being an only child. She'd simply accepted it as the way it was.

But sometimes, when she'd looked at her parents and witnessed a look pass between them, she'd feel left out. Like the proverbial third wheel.

And in her awkwardness, she'd attempted to be a little louder to get their notice.

But, of course, her noise and fussing hadn't created the results she'd craved. Actually, all that had happened was she got sent to her room.

In no time, Ella and Loyal reached the farm. Unable to stop herself, she scanned the yard, looking for changes. There were many.

"You've been busy," she said. "Why, you've whitewashed the barn and weeded all the flower beds."

"I've been making my brothers come over to help." Looking as eager as a child, he stepped toward the front door. "Would you . . . I mean, do you want to see how the finished floors turned out?"

"Of course."

He held the door open as she walked

inside. But the moment her foot touched the smooth planks, now stained a dark cherry red, she couldn't contain her gasp. "Oh, Loyal, everything looks so different!"

"It's the floor . . ."

"Look how much whiter the walls are!"

"I painted those, too."

She turned, noticed that the curtains that her mother had made for the kitchen had been taken down. Now only shiny white window frame and a clean, bright window appeared over the sink.

"The curtains are gone."

"Yes," he sputtered. "They were pretty, but not really to my taste."

She'd always thought those curtains were ugly. Actually, she'd never seen the need for them in such an open house surrounded by land. "Whose taste do you think they were?" she asked, doing her best to keep her expression earnest and thoughtful.

Right in front of her, Loyal looked positively tongue-tied. "Well, I don't know—"

Feeling sorry for him, she pressed her hand to his arm. "I'm teasin', Loyal. I never liked those curtains."

"Truly?"

She nodded. "Truly."

"Whew. It's nerve-racking, not knowing how to act. I want to show off the changes, but I don't want to hurt your feelings."

"Loyal, I've told you that I would've liked to have made changes. I just wasn't able."

"Yes, but those changes were your ideas, not mine."

"I like your changes. I promise." With a bit of a shock, she realized that she still held her hand on his arm. And that she was standing too close to him.

Her eyes widened. Just as he slowly reached out and held her waist. Not hard. Gently. To hold her in place.

Her breath hitched. No man had ever held her before. And now she couldn't imagine another man's embrace ever feeling so right.

Their eyes met. His eyes flickered. A new awareness entered in them, and it had nothing to do with pity or worry or being a protector.

It all had to do with being a man and a woman together and the awareness that came from being alone. It had to do with attraction and desire and all the things she'd dreamed about but had at times resigned herself to thinking that those things might never happen for her.

Loyal swallowed. Ella found herself watching the muscles in his neck shift and move.

Noticed a faint band of perspiration on his brow.

And for just a split second, she imagined stepping closer to him, finally kissing him. The two of them declaring their love.

All such foolish, foolish things.

With a start, she stepped back. "I should probably get on my way."

Loyal mirrored her movements, stepping back, too. "Oh. Yes. Of course. I'll take you back right now."

She turned and walked out in a rush, feeling her cheeks heat, her feet stumble.

Because all she wanted was to feel his touch again. To feel, for one more moment, that she was a woman. A pretty woman. Worth his time.

Worth everything.

Chapter 22

"So how is Jenna? How was your time at the arts-and-crafts fair?" Mattie asked, feeling proud of herself. Why, she sounded truly concerned and interested. Terribly friendlike.

Graham shrugged as he stretched his legs in the back of the van. He'd elected to go with her to the doctor when Lucy had bowed out suddenly, saying she'd caught a bug and wasn't feeling too well.

Though Mattie hadn't minded going alone, she would be lying if she said she wasn't thankful for Graham's companionship.

"Jenna is fine. She seemed to enjoy the craft fair."

"That's all the information you're going to share? Come on, Graham. Surely even you can spare me a few more details!"

"Even me?"

"You, Graham Weaver, are notoriously closemouthed."

"There's not much to tell," he finally said. "Jenna walked by my side and we looked at the quilts."

"And?"

"And what?"

"Did you enjoy being with her?"

"I did. Well, somewhat."

"What happened?" She thought for a moment. "You didn't start talking about cows and horses and goats did you?"

A muscle in his cheek jumped. "What if I did?"

"No one wants to hear about the antics of barnyard animals."

"You do."

"Well, I'm different."

"To answer your question, no. I most certainly did not start telling Jenna about Bridgett. But I'm sure if I had, she would have been most entertained. Bridgett is a most entertaining cow."

"She's still a cow, Graham." Growing more curious, she said softly, "What happened?"

"Nothing. We talked. She smiled. I enjoy being around her. We made plans for me to visit her at her home one evening next week."

"But?"

"You know me too well, don't you?" he said dryly.

"You could say that." Some would say she knew him best of all.

With enough drama to appear on the stage, he sighed. "All right, Miss Nosypants, here's the problem. She bored me. Though I did talk to her about the chickens"—he held up a hand to stop her teasing—"and about my intention to apply for work at the garage-door factory this fall, she wasn't too interested in either subject."

"What did she want to talk about?"

He shrugged. "Mattie, I have no idea. Most of the time, we just looked at the art and commented on the weather. It was a long evening."

Delight raced through her. With effort, she tried to tamp it down. "Truly?"

"You sound happy about it."

"I'm not happy," she said as all too soon Charlie pulled up to the circular drive in front of the medical center.

"You sound happy," Graham countered as they got out, waved goodbye to Charlie, and stepped into the air-conditioned lobby of the medical center.

As the cold air fanned her cheeks, all their jokes slipped away and the focus of their day fell on her shoulders.

The weight of it felt overwhelming. Mattie steeled her spine. "It's, uh, this way."

"Hey," Graham said, "are you all right? Do you want to wait a moment before we go in?"

"Of course not. Besides, more often than not I have to wait for a long time."

Looking her over, his expression held none of the amusement that had made the ride seem so short. "Is there a purpose for this visit? You never said."

"Yes. It's . . . . the purpose is to give me the results of the latest biopsy."

"You didn't tell me you had another one."

"I know."

His touch stopped her. "Mattie, what happens if it's bad news?"

"If it's cancer?" At his nod, she flinched. "I don't know."

"All right, then. Let's go hear the news."

Suddenly, she was afraid. "Graham, I fear I must warn you—at these appointments . . . I'm not always at my best."

As he opened the doctor's door, his expression changed, turning as amused as ever. "Not to worry, Mattie. I'm used to that."

Dorothy knocked after 9:00 that evening. The moment Ella opened the door, Dorothy marched in, purpose emanating with every step.

For a moment, Ella considered asking her to leave. The feelings of warmth and friendship she'd once felt for Dorothy were fading away. Now, it seemed, there was only a lack of trust.

Well, she *felt* a lack of trust.

"What is it that you want, Dorothy?"

"That's all you have to say?"

"It's not. But it might be all that is suitable to talk about this evening."

Without being asked, Dorothy sat. Temper simmering, Ella watched her friend's face as she visibly attempted to get the best of the situation.

As the seconds passed, Ella realized her patience had passed as well. "Dorothy, why are you here?"

"I wanted to talk to you."

"I'm listening. But only for another two minutes. Then it will be time for you to go."

"All right." She sighed. "Ella, why have you left me?"

"You need to explain yourself."

"When I offered you this place to stay and put in my recommendation for the job, you promised you were grateful."

"I am."

"But you haven't shown it. Why, you haven't acted appreciative at all! Instead of spending time with me—like you promised—you've been darting off with other people."

"Dorothy, we've already talked about this. I am paying you rent. I am working at the library. While it is true you did much for me, it is also true that I don't owe you anything."

Her face grew darker. "You sent the bishop to talk to me."

"I spoke to him about your actions. He was the one who wanted to speak with you."

"Because you made up lies about me."

"You have been entering my home un-invited and went through my trash. That dinner was rotten, Dorothy."

"If you had been with me when I cooked it, you would have liked it."

"But what you are doing makes no sense! Why in the world would you do such a thing? You had to know actions like that would only make me want to pull further away from you."

"Ella," she said softly. "You don't un-derstand. All my life, I've lived on the out-side. My family left me. Then my boyfriend rejected me. Since then, I've been only by myself. And then we became friends."

Her voice turned softer, sweeter as she looked beyond Ella to a place where her memories laid. "Do you remember the first time we met? You had just left the optical shop and were fingering your new eye-glasses. I told you they looked nice. And you, Ella, said thank you, and that no one had ever complimented you on your glasses before."

That had been four years ago. Back before her parents had passed away and all Ella could think about was herself. She'd been seventeen and aching to be smaller framed and smaller in size.

It had been a Monday, she knew, because she'd also still been smarting from Corrine's news. She and Peter had announced their engagement at church the day before.

And instead of feeling happy for her best friend, she'd been overcome with jealousy.

She'd spent the entire time at the singing eyeing Loyal Weaver and the way he'd had smiles for all the girls . . . except for her.

Ella realized now that the reason he hadn't smiled at her had been because she hadn't smiled at anyone that evening. She'd been so shy, so worried about saying the wrong things, that she'd kept to herself. And so, of course, everyone had kept their distance.

Yes, back then, she'd had a child's view of the world—a selfish way of thinking, filtering everything done and said around her through an insecure haze. And Dorothy, being ten years older, had fed her insecurities and doubts.

Now Ella was starting to realize that Dorothy had wanted her to also be alone. That far from giving, she'd been taking from Ella—all in the hopes that Ella would fulfill her own selfish desires.

"I remember that day, well," she murmured. "I was so grateful for your compliment about my new frames." Oh, how self-centered and insecure she'd been! Now her vanity shamed her.

Dorothy stood up. "Then you must also remember how happy you were to have me. You needed me. You needed a friend."

She had appreciated Dorothy's friendship, but their relationship wasn't near as one-sided as Dorothy was painting it. "You needed a friend, too."

"We still need each other. I'm sure of it. Ella, you might think that you have a lot in common with your other friends, but you don't. People like Corrine won't stick around."

"Of course she will. Corrine and I have been friends for years."

"But she's married. You likely never will be."

The harsh statement stung. And now

that she had her job and was learning to reach out to other people more, Ella felt sure, with God's help, she would meet her perfect man. "Of course I will, Dorothy."

"No one is going to want you, Ella." Looking her over pityingly, Dorothy said, "Surely you don't think someone like Loyal Weaver is going to court you. Do you?"

Right then and there, old worries and doubts rushed forward, nearly drowning her new attitude.

And then, to her amazement, Ella thought of Katie. And that's when she realized— remembered—that merely being "good enough" for someone wasn't what she wanted. She wanted to be as strong and willful as that little girl. She wanted to learn to push in order to get her way.

"Whether Loyal becomes my beau or not is none of your concern."

"It is. I had plans for us. You were sup- posed to always be there for me. You are going to be just like me one day."

"No, I'm not. What did the bishop say?"

She turned away. "About what you might expect. He reminded me of my position in our community. He talked about friendship and prayer." Looking back at Ella, pure scorn and derision mottled her cheeks. "But he knows nothing."

"Dorothy, you should listen to him."

"I know Joseph. I've known him for years. And I remember when he wasn't the *bishop,* but merely a young man doing foolish things." She lifted her chin. "He once got caught having a buggy race late at night. I reminded him of that."

"And what did he do?"

"Oh, he pretended it was nonsense, and a long time ago. But I reminded him that our past never leaves us. We are who we are. I am always going to be too outspoken and smart for most of the people in our community." She lowered her voice. "And you, Ella, are always going to be too tall and plain for the likes of the man you want."

Ella shook her head. *"Nee."*

Dorothy stepped forward, her expression earnest. "Don't you understand, Ella? You can rush forward and make a fool of yourself, but you can never ignore the past. It's always there, like a light on the back of a buggy. It's always there, shining like a remembrance. Making sure you will never forget."

Walking to the door, Ella opened it. "It's time you left."

"I'll leave, but promise me that you'll take heed to my warnings?"

"I cannot do that."

Dorothy turned to face her. "Why won't you listen to me?"

Gripping the edge of the door, Ella said, "For the first time, I think I'm hearing *everything* you have to say, loud and clear. This is my two week notice. I'll be leaving here soon."

"You can't."

Dorothy spoke with such certainty, it almost made Ella smile. What did she think Ella was going to do? Listen to her and meekly follow directions?

"Of course I will."

"We have a contract."

"No, we don't. And even if we did, you would have to agree that you have already broken our agreement when you violated my privacy." As Dorothy continued to stare at her in shock, Ella said, "It must be obvious to you now. You can't shape me into the person you'd hoped I would be."

"I never wanted to mold you. I only wanted you to be the person you pretended to be. The person you said you were . . . which you are not."

"I am sorry, but I'm afraid that's not going to happen."

"You'll regret this."

"Perhaps. But it is time you left."

"I want you out before two weeks' time. I want you out of here, out of my home, as soon as possible."

"I'll do my best to leave quickly."

"It won't be soon enough." One last, malevolent look punctuated her face before she turned, opened the door with a jerk, and left.

But instead of feeling relief that Dorothy was gone, Ella now felt even more scared. She was completely alone, and because of that, more vulnerable than ever.

Ella was starting to realize that Dorothy was even more dangerous when she couldn't be seen than when she was in plain sight.

An edgy sense of foreboding flowed

through Ella. And as she turned the dead-bolt on the front door, she considered propping a chair against it, too.

Fear. She now feared Dorothy. She feared Dorothy more than she feared for an uncertain future.

Chapter 23

"Waiting for Ella again, are you?" John asked from the other side of the counter.

Loyal felt his cheeks heat. "I guess it's pretty obvious?"

"Only to a man who's done some waiting a time or two for a woman." With a wink he added, "Of course, the way you're sitting in front of the picture window like a puppy in a pet store gave me a hint as well."

With effort, Loyal turned away from his spot, realizing his uncle was exactly right. He had been sitting somewhat like an expectant pup, hoping for a smile from someone special.

Around the small dining area, all the men who'd overheard were grinning, too.

"Don't fret, Loyal," Bishop Thomas said with a smirk. "We've all done it. Sooner or later each man finds he can't take his eyes off a woman . . ."

"And it's up to the rest of us to make note of it and tease him," Henry said.

"I know I have," John murmured.

Uncle John was truly a surprise, Loyal reflected. Once Amish, now English, he'd had a successful business in Indiana, then packed everything up and moved out to Jacob's Crossing just a few months ago.

Now, here he was, owning his own do-nut shop in the middle of Amish country. Being a part of the network of friends and acquaintances but also not.

And now here Loyal was learning that his uncle had waited on a woman before. "Are you talking about Angela?"

"I am not. I have dated some since she divorced me, you know."

It felt strange to hear him talk about divorce so easily. Even the thought of di-vorce made Loyal uneasy. "I'm glad you haven't been alone." Then, all the sudden, he remembered seeing his uncle and an unfamiliar woman walking together. "Are you seeing anyone now?"

"No."

"Really?"

His uncle gazed through the thick glass window. "Well, I suppose I am. Kind of." He shrugged, looking completely perplexed. "Anyway, my point is that I know that look of yours. We all do. And you, my nephew, are looking head over heels."

Though it was on the tip of his tongue to deny it, he sighed. "I guess I have been waiting for Ella. She's become a *gut* friend."

"From what your mother has told me, it sounds like Ella could use some good friends right now."

"Uncle John, do you think it would have been possible for you to have known that things weren't going to work out between you and Angela?"

John's expression became shuttered.

Loyal felt horrible. He shouldn't have brought up the past like that. They all knew John's failed marriage was a source of discomfort for him. "Sorry. I shouldn't have pried."

"You didn't," John said. "I was just wondering if I could have known what the future had in store for me."

Even the bishop was leaning forward, all ears. "And?"

"And, the answer is, I'm not sure." Picking up a rag, John began to wipe down the already clean countertop. "Angela and I should never have married in the first place. We were too different. It was soon very obvious that I was never going to be who she wanted." Looking from the bishop to Loyal, he said, "You have to remember, when I first met Angela, I was young. Only eighteen."

"You'd just left us," the bishop said.

"I had. It was a really hard time for me," John admitted. "I had a chip on my shoulder, and was so angry."

Loyal hadn't heard this story before. "Angry at what?"

"Angry at the *Englischers*, for not giving me a welcome party I guess," he said dryly.

"What are you talking about?"

"Leaving the faith had been such a big step for me, I thought everyone would give me slack. But they didn't. All the men my age just made fun of me when I didn't fit in." He rolled his eyes. "And believe me, I stuck out in a lot of ways. I did some really foolish things." He took a deep breath, then averted his eyes. "I was also very angry at myself. Because I thought I'd made a mistake, but I didn't know how to fix it."

"You should have come back to us," the bishop said.

"Perhaps . . . but even if I had wanted to, my pride wouldn't let me. I wanted to be independent." Removing a half-filled coffee-pot, he checked the time, poured out what was in the carafe, and started making a fresh pot. "Anyway, it was right then and there that I first met Angela. She was my boss's daughter, and pretty much the first person who didn't act like I was a source of amusement."

"So, she wasn't a complete mistake. She was the right person for you at that time," Loyal said.

"In a way, I suppose she was," John said as he filled a paper liner with coffee grounds. "She made me happy, and I loved that. And she was beautiful—and I was young enough to like that very much, too. But then, well, she realized that I could never be who she wanted; and when I found out she was seeing another man, I realized I could never stay married to a woman who cheated on me."

"What happened to her? Do you know?"

Uncle John nodded. "I came across her name on the computer when I was traveling here. She's married and has a family. So I guess she finally did find what she was looking for."

"Well, I for one, am glad you're back here," Bishop Thomas said.

"I am, too." He cleared his throat. "Well, this is what I get for asking you a personal question, isn't it, Loyal? I get nosy, and end up telling you about myself."

"It was the right time."

A look of understanding crossed his features, softening them. "I think so." Then his smile grew wide. "And here comes Ella, walking right by here. And, if I'm not mistaken, I think she just looked in here at you."

Loyal's heart jumped. "You think so?" he asked, getting to his feet.

"I saw it, too, Loyal," the bishop said gruffly. "It would be a mighty *gut* idea if you went out and caught her. You know, before she walked on by and didn't think you cared."

He edged closer to the door, feeling like a silly fool. "John? Do you think we have enough in common?"

"I think you two have the potential to have as much in common as you possibly want," he said. "That is, if you go see her."

Loyal opened the door and strode out, the men's laughter spurring him forward.

"Ella! Ella, wait, would you?"

He was coming her way! With effort, she schooled her features to something a little calmer.

"Good morning, Loyal Weaver," she said. "Having another donut?"

He looked at his empty hands and chuckled. "Actually, I was so busy speaking with my uncle and Bishop Thomas that I forgot to eat."

"How are they this morning?"

"They are good. Would you like to go inside for a bit? Or are you off to work?"

"Actually, I'm not working for another two hours. I just was eager for a break." After quickly debating whether to burden Loyal with her latest news, she added, "And I thought I'd try to find a new place to live."

"New? What happened?"

"Dorothy, she was very upset about the

bishop stopping by. She wants me to move as soon as possible."

"That's hardly fair."

"At first I was upset, but a part of me is kind of relieved," she admitted as they walked past the library, and then by mutual consent, down a walking path to the Crossing Park.

As the path narrowed and they moved a bit closer to each other, she lowered her voice. "Loyal, I don't think she's quite right in the head. Her anger was scary, and I'm afraid that the way she looks at me makes me on edge. I'm now worried about coming home, wondering what she's been doing in my absence."

A fierce protectiveness rushed through him. Ella was such a sweet person, he ached with the thought that Dorothy was using those good qualities against her.

"Do you fear for your safety?" he murmured. There were a lot of things he wanted to say. He wanted to promise her that everything was going to be just fine. That he could solve all her problems. But of course, he couldn't.

"I'm not afraid. Yet."

"Yet," Loyal echoed, then, almost without

thinking, he wrapped an arm around her shoulders. For a second, she tensed, then he felt the muscles in her shoulders relax, and finally she moved closer to him.

That action filled him with happiness. Ella had been too alone for too long. He wanted to support her.

"Did you sleep last night?"

"Some. Mainly, I just kept going over that conversation, wondering how I could have handled things better." She bit her lip. "Loyal, Dorothy is angrier than ever."

"I'm sorry to hear that."

Dealing with too many emotions to handle both walking and talking, she stopped and faced him. "I'm worried she's going to ask me to leave the library." Tears pricked her eyes as she recalled the pain Dorothy's threats had caused her. "I love working at the library. I love being around the *kinner.*"

"Oh, Ella. I am terribly sorry. We will get through this." His gaze was sweet as he reached out and rubbed her other shoulder.

"It's not your problem . . ."

"It is, because it involves you," he said softly.

Then, before she really knew what had

happened, he opened his embrace, and she stepped closer. Then finally pressed her face into the nook of his shoulder.

And sighed as his arms wrapped around her and held her close. Into a very sweet, very comforting embrace.

Another pair of tears trailed down her cheeks, embarrassing her. Well, they would have embarrassed her if they hadn't been completely alone and her face wasn't pressed against his shoulder.

"It's okay, Ella," he murmured, patting her back slightly. "I promise, I'll help you make everything fine again."

She believed him. Slowly, she lifted her arms, too, and wrapped them around him.

Everything she was now feeling had nothing to do with fear and comfort and everything to do with a longing so fierce that it was almost a tangible thing.

This was Loyal Weaver she was embracing—the boy she used to watch from a distance, the man she used to dream about. Loyal Weaver, who to her was always so charming, so handsome, so everything!

She closed her eyes and inhaled.

And then felt his lips brush her brow.

She lifted her head. *"Danke,"* she murmured. "Thank you for believing in me."

"Don't thank me for that." His blue gaze felt like a caress. "I'm glad to be here for you." His right hand reached up and brushed the back of two fingers against her cheek. "Please don't cry anymore. I hate to see your tears."

"I'll try not to." Her voice drifted off as his head inched closer. His hand still on her cheek, she felt completely comforted.

Her lips parted. Trying to think of something to say. Something to tell him, about how much he meant to her. About how grateful she was to him—

But then she thought of nothing as his lips brushed hers. As he kissed her.

Ella's breath hitched. A thousand thoughts ran through her head. But then nothing else really mattered as she tilted her head and kissed him back. Right there. In the park. Surely God was very, very good. If he could make her girlish dreams turn into this reality, then surely He could make anything possible.

Chapter 24

The problem with being Katie Weaver, was that everyone always assumed she only wanted something to eat.

"Katie, you must eat your breakfast. It's getting cold," her mother chided from across the kitchen.

"I'm not hungry."

Her mother stared at her for a long moment, then briskly walked over and pressed her palm to Katie's head. "You don't feel feverish. What hurts?"

"Nothing, Mamm. I just ain't hungry." Before her mother could start fretting about wasting food, Katie scrambled to her feet.

"I want to go see Ella today. Can you take me soon?"

"Is that why you are not hungry? Because you're so anxious to see the librarian?"

"Ella is more than the librarian. She's my friend."

With a sigh, her mother sat down at the table, picked up a fork, and started spearing Katie's untouched pan-fried potatoes. "I know that, dear. But to be honest, I don't understand your interest in her all that much. Why does she hold such fascination for you?"

"Because she's nice. And she loves books, too."

After taking a few more bites, her mother looked at her fondly. "I suppose that's enough, *jah*?"

"I want to be a librarian, too," Katie said, realizing right as she said the words that that was the truth. She loved reading and loved books, all books.

And unlike the people in her family, who were busy, busy, busy . . . Ella Hostetler understood Katie's need to always have a book to read.

Even if she couldn't read all that well yet.

"My. Well, I have to say you might have already discovered what future God has intended for you. It seems as if being a librarian would be a wonderful-*gut* occupation for my dear daughter."

Katie's heart beat faster. "You mean it, Mamm?"

"Indeed I do. I've always thought you could be anything you wanted to be." She blinked, looking out into the distance. "I had imagined you would take after me, and would want to be a wife and mother. But perhaps there's a lot of your father in you, too."

They hardly ever talked about her *daed*. "Daed wanted to be a librarian, too?"

Her mother laughed. "*Nee,* child. Your father always enjoyed a *gut buch.* I suppose you take after him."

"So, can I go see Ella today?"

"I don't know, dear. I have a lot to do."

Looking toward the door, Katie knew where to go next. "I'll go ask Loyal to take me."

"I doubt he'll have time."

"Why? Is he already out in the fields?"

"*Nee,* he's working in the barn some. But, Katie, your brother has far more to do than to run you places in the buggy."

"Maybe . . . or maybe not. Loyal always seems to have time to see Ella."

"Katie, you shouldn't gossip like that," her mother admonished. But after biting her lip for a moment, she said, "But do you think Loyal is fond of Ella?"

"Oh, *jah!*" Katie said, standing very tall and proud. It wasn't often she knew something her mother didn't. "You should see them together, Mamm. When Loyal is next to Ella, he stares at her all the time."

"You shouldn't say such things. . . . But, truly?"

"Uh-huh."

Amusement flashed in her mother's eyes; then with a sigh, she said, "Yes, Katie, you may go ask your brother if he will take you to the library."

"Danke!"

"Wait!"

Katie skidded to a stop.

"You may go . . . after you eat some of your breakfast."

Eyeing the plate, Katie grimaced. "But it's cold now."

"That's the consequence, *jah*? Little girls who don't eat their hot breakfasts must eat it cold."

With her feet feeling like lead, Katie walked back to the table and sat back down. Another glance at her mother warned her against arguing further.

With a sigh, she scooped up a forkful of eggs. Experience had told her that there was only so much her mother would put up with.

"I can't believe you talked me into taking you to the library this morning," Loyal said to his little sister. "Remind me to ignore you next time you come into the barn."

Katie fidgeted next to him. A casual observer would think she was ashamed of her nagging. Or perhaps embarrassed to be caught being so headstrong. But he knew better. So far, Katie hadn't met a situation that could embarrass her. "That's not very nice, Loyal," she finally muttered.

For a brief moment, he considered apologizing—but if he did, he knew his tiny sister with her very big mouth would twist and turn his words into something else entirely.

So, he kept on the offensive. "It wasn't terribly nice of you to interrupt my work."

She darted another sly look his way. "One day I'll be old enough to drive the buggy into town."

"That is true." Against his will, he thought about Katie growing up. And then, perversely, the idea of it made him sad. From the day she was born, their little Katie had made them all laugh with her antics and dramatics.

As they stopped at a traffic light, she looked at him again. "Or maybe one day I won't have to drive to the library to see Ella."

"Where else would she be?"

"Maybe she'll live closer." A hint of a smile lit her face. "A whole lot closer?"

"Why do you say that?" Against his will, Loyal felt embarrassment overtake him and his cheeks heat. Just like a teenager!

Surely Katie hadn't heard about his kiss?

"Oh, no reason . . ."

"You know something," he retorted. "What do you know?"

"Just that you like her."

The light turned green and he motioned the buggy forward. Thankful for something to occupy the majority of his attention, he murmured, "Why do you say that?"

"Come on, Loyal. It's not hard to tell."

"Because?"

"Because you look at her all moony, that's why."

Before he remembered to be far more mature, he snapped, "And just how does 'moony' look?"

Katie's mouth opened, she looked at him; then, surely seeing something foreboding on his face, shut her mouth again. "Nothing."

"Come now, Katie. Now's no time to stop. Explain yourself."

"It's just . . . I just think when you look at her, you smile with your eyes."

Loyal swallowed hard. Luckily, he'd just pulled up to the library. No sooner had he halted the buggy than Katie looked ready to scramble out of the conveyance. "Hold, now. I'm comin' in, too."

"You don't have to."

"I certainly do! How else do you think you would get home?"

With a hand on her shoulder, he guided her through the main doors of the library.

Only then did he realize Katie's arms were filled with three picture books.

A handful of ladies behind the main counter looked up when they entered. Ella was one of them. Her cheeks bloomed bright and her lips parted.

Which only made him think of kissing her again.

"Ella! Me and Loyal came to see you!" Katie said, far too exuberantly.

A few patrons glared at the pint-sized disturbance. "You must be quieter, Katie," Loyal warned.

"It's all right," Ella said as she walked around the desk to greet them. "I'm glad you came here to visit. What a wonderful-*gut* surprise! So, are you ready for stars on your reading chart?"

"I wanted to see you. I mean, we both did," Katie said with an unusually awkward look toward Loyal. "Are you reading stories today?"

She shook her head. "I'm afraid not." Meeting Loyal's gaze, she stumbled over her next words. "Actually, I'm not sure if I'm going to be working here much longer."

Loyal felt his chest constrict as he saw her lip tremble. "What happened?"

After glancing behind her, she motioned them to the side. "Jayne. I mean *Ms. Donovan*—she was mighty upset with me today. We had to talk. Dorothy . . . Dorothy has been spreading lies about me."

"Katie, leave us for a few minutes, please," Loyal said quickly.

His sister froze. "But—"

"Katie, let me visit with Ella for a moment in private. It's important."

With a wounded look, she left them and went to the juvenile stacks.

The moment they were alone, Ella's shoulders relaxed and her bottom lip trembled. "I don't know how, but I think Dorothy saw us kissing, Loyal," she whispered.

"How could she?"

"I have no idea. But . . . but she told Ms. Donovan that my morals were loose and that I was losing my apartment."

"But that's her doing!"

"I know, but the way Ms. Donovan heard it, Dorothy made me sound like the very worst sort of person. We were just discussing whether or not she wants me to continue here."

"That's not right. I'll go speak with Ms.

Donovan." He paused, thinking of who was to blame. "Or Dorothy."

"I'd rather you didn't. This is something I need to take care of on my own."

He didn't agree. He wanted to help her. At the very least, he could be by her side when she confronted the other woman.

But he also knew he had no right. "Are you sure?"

She swallowed. "I'm going to go home and talk to Dorothy. Things will only get better once I straighten everything out once and for all."

"How about I drive you?"

"*Nee,* Loyal. This time I want to take care of myself. It will be better this way." Reaching for his hand, she lightly squeezed. "So if you could, as soon as I visit with Katie for a few minutes, I'd be grateful if you could be on your way."

The pain in her eyes broke his heart. "All right, then."

After two steps toward the children's section, she stopped. "Oh, and Loyal—"

He searched her face, waiting for a change of heart. "Yes?"

"*Danke.* Thank you for caring."

"You're welcome," he said, though his

reply felt completely inadequate. "Ella, I care about you."

Her lips curved. "I know," she said before turning away.

Fifteen minutes later, as Loyal held Katie's hand on the sidewalk toward the buggy, he realized that saying he was sorry seemed terribly inadequate. Ella was so sweet, and had already given up so much for her mother. Now, here, when she was just discovering what a wonderful woman she was, Dorothy was threatening to make her lose everything all over again.

And when they were driving the buggy home, Katie reading her new book by his side, Loyal also knew that he didn't just *care* for Ella. No, what he felt for her was far stronger.

Fact was, she had already claimed his heart.

"Katie, I do believe we need to go back," he said suddenly.

"To the library?"

Loyal nodded. "I can't let Ella solve her problem by herself." And with that, he turned the buggy and headed back to the library.

He sincerely hoped he wasn't too late.

Chapter 25

"John, please say you still have some long johns covered with chocolate frosting," Mattie called out the moment she entered the front door of the Kaffi Haus.

As a pair of men looked up from their newspapers, frowned, then went back to reading, John rested his elbows on the glass countertop and smiled in amusement. "It's been that kind of a day, huh?"

"You don't know the half of it. Graham accompanied me to the doctor yesterday."

"How did it go?"

She loved how Graham's Uncle John was always so calm and nonjudgmental.

Everything seemed to go along on its own time with him.

"I'll tell you about it over a donut. If you have the time."

He looked around at the empty dining room. "I might be able to spare a moment or two. I just made a fresh pot of coffee. Want a cup with your long johns?"

She almost cheered, she was so happy to hear that he had more than one of her favorite donuts available. "Yes, please."

"Coming right up, then. Have a seat, dear."

With a relieved sigh, she sat at the smallest table, in the corner, the exact opposite of where most patrons sat. But she yearned for peace and quiet.

Well, at least a little bit of privacy.

In less than two minutes, John appeared. "Here we go, Mattie. Two donuts and one cup of coffee."

She noticed the creamy milky color and sighed with happiness. "And you even put a lot of cream in it. Thank you."

"Any time. Eat up for a moment, and then I'll be right back."

Ah, but the first taste of the long john was always something close to heaven.

She closed her eyes and took a moment to enjoy the rich chocolatyness of the pastry.

Two sips of coffee later, John came back and sat in the chair across from her. "Now, tell me. What happened?"

"I got the results back from my latest biopsy."

The lines in his jaw tensed. "And?"

"And I don't have cancer," she said in a rush.

"This is going to sound strange, but for some reason, I don't think you seem happy about that."

"I'm stunned, I think." Almost grudgingly, she admitted, "Graham said the same thing."

"Is there a reason you're surprised?"

After popping the last of the first donut in her mouth, she carefully wiped her mouth. "I'm afraid so," she admitted. "I've been in such a bad place emotionally, I couldn't imagine a life without cancer."

"You were afraid to hope for something better."

She looked at him in surprise. "You understand," she said, surprised.

He laughed. "I know it's hard to imagine that an old guy like me could understand . . .

but I do. See, I've had circumstances much like yours."

"Have you had cancer?"

His eyes widened in surprise, then he shuttered his expression quickly. "No, nothing like that. But I suffered losses. Some of which were painful," he said quietly.

Mattie stayed silent. For reasons she couldn't explain, she felt a connection with John Weaver, stronger than she'd felt with anyone in years, except maybe Graham. Though she didn't want to be rude, she was curious about what hardships he'd faced.

After sipping his coffee, John propped one foot on his opposite knee. "I'm sure you know years ago I left here."

"You didn't want to be Amish."

His eyebrows rose at her bluntness, then he nodded. "No, I didn't. My brother, he did everything right. I thought I couldn't measure up." Staring at Mattie, he shrugged. "Now I wonder why that mattered so much. Anyway, I left here to the farthest place I could afford, which was Indianapolis." His gaze turned sardonic. "I thought it was terribly exotic."

"A big city would be."

"It was," he said softly. "Anyway, leaving

Geauga County was the hardest thing I ever did—to leave the order and make a life on my own."

"But you did . . ."

"I did at that."

"And you got married?"

"I did. And after two years, I divorced."

The notion of ending a marriage was foreign to Mattie. "You didn't want to honor your wedding vows?"

"Oh, I did. Angela didn't." Bitterness crept into his voice. "She found someone else and left."

Understanding dawned. "So that's why you say things have happened out of your control."

He nodded. "I was Amish enough to think that I would have worked long and hard before I would have accepted a divorce. Angela, however, went ahead and left me little choice in the matter. She was gone and had made it plain that she wasn't going to come back to me, ever." He sighed. "Anyway, for twenty years, I told myself, it was what I deserved. I left my family and attempted to form a new life. But you can't, you know? We are all a product of our past.

No matter how hard we might wish otherwise, that truth remains the same."

"Now I can officially say I am cancer-free, but I hardly know how to act. I'm afraid to move on."

"I was that way, too, Mattie. I stayed away, afraid to imagine I could go back. Afraid that wouldn't be welcomed. Afraid to return. But Calvin's visit spurred me into action."

"And now you own this donut shop."

"I do." Looking around, his expression turned bemused. "I wouldn't have thought it, but this place suits me."

"Do you think you'll ever find love again?"

"A year ago, I would have told you no. But lately, I'm starting to think maybe there's hope for me yet." He raised his coffee cup and gave her a toast in the air. "And I'm here to tell you, Mattie, that if there's hope for me after twenty years, perhaps there's hope for you, too."

"Perhaps," she echoed. But she was afraid to admit to anything. What if she gave herself hope and then discovered that she'd been a fool, all over again?

Behind them, the door chimed.

John got to his feet with a faint groan, then instantly became more on edge.

Curious, Mattie turned to look at the newcomer and noticed it was Mary Zehr, the widow who lived on a farm on the opposite side of Jacob's Crossing.

"Mary, hello," John said, every muscle in his face suddenly still.

"John," Mary murmured. "It's *gut* to see you."

But Mattie noticed she didn't look at the pastries in the glass case once. No, all she was doing was staring at John.

And John's expression was as tender as she'd ever seen it.

Suddenly, the air in the restaurant became thick with tension. And Mattie felt like there were too many people in the near-empty space. With a flick of her wrist, she wrapped the last half of her second long john in a napkin, grabbed her Styrofoam cup, and walked out of the restaurant.

She smiled when neither John nor Mary ever looked her way.

As she stood on the sidewalk, she decided she might as well take a walk. And headed to the library.

But what she found there was a scene of

chaos. Ella was nowhere to be found, little Katie Weaver was crying, and Ms. Donovan, standing with an arm around Katie's shoulders, looked to be in tears herself. Off to the side was Loyal, looking as if his whole world had just come tumbling down.

Mattie rushed over to the women. "What's wrong?"

"Everything," Katie wailed, in that usual headstrong way of hers.

Though Mattie knew Graham sometimes became exasperated with his little sister's outspoken ways, today she was very grateful for Katie's propensity to speak her mind. "Such as?"

"Miss Ella, she left and she's probably never going to come back here, neither."

Mattie was completely confused. "I find that hard to believe."

Finally Ms. Donovan spoke. "This morning, Ella spoke to me. She was finding it difficult to work here."

"Why?"

"Because of the other librarian," Katie blurted. "The mean one."

Mattie had learned to trust Katie. "Who?" she asked, certain she was going to get the unvarnished truth.

Finally Loyal spoke. "Dorothy has been spreading rumors about Ella. She's been whispering them to Ms. Donovan and upsetting Ella greatly."

"I wish she had more faith in herself," Ms. Donovan said. "If she would have given me more time to talk to her, I would have told her that none of Dorothy's stories had any bearing on her job. I think Ella is doing a fine job, and I really thought she fit in here."

"Where is she now?" Mattie asked, looking from Loyal to Ms. Donovan.

"She went to try to straighten things out with Dorothy," Loyal said.

"Do you think she'll have any luck?"

"Nee," Katie blurted. "Dorothy didn't want her to work here, or even live in her house."

Mattie was floored. "All this is so hard to understand."

"Lies like hers usually are," Loyal said quietly.

Jayne Donovan shook her head sadly. "I'm not exactly sure of the whole story," she said apologetically. With a wave of her hand, she added, "For some reason, Dorothy thinks Ella has loose morals."

His face red, Loyal said, "She only said that because she saw me kiss Ella."

Shaking her head sadly, Mattie said, "Loyal, we need to go help her."

"I think you're right, though I did promise Ella that I would let her speak to Dorothy on her own."

"Well, you did let her have time to speak with Dorothy. Now I think we should go check on her."

"Are you sure you're up to this? I don't want you overdoing it."

"I'm perfectly healthy now," she said, realizing how extremely glad she was about that. "More than anything, I want to try to help Ella." Mattie knew helping her friend would be good for her heart and soul, too. For so long, she'd only been thinking about her own needs and failings. Now God was giving her a chance to actually help someone else.

She couldn't help but grab hold of the opportunity.

Turning to Ms. Donovan, Loyal said, "I hate to ask this of you, but is there any way you could let Katie stay here for a little while? I'd hate for her to be any more embroiled in this than she already is."

Ms. Donovan looked at Katie and smiled. "I don't think we'll have any trouble staying here and keeping occupied. Katie, would you like to see the brand-new picture books that just came in?"

Katie's eyes widened. "Oh, yes."

Loyal smiled in obvious relief. "All right, then. Mattie, let's go see if we can find Ella and offer her some support. I don't want her to be alone."

With a wave, Mattie left the library by Loyal's side, scurrying down the sidewalk as she did her best to keep up with his long-legged stride.

And that's when she realized with some surprise that for the first time in a long while, no one mentioned her cancer.

They'd moved on.

And that gave her the strength to move on, too. She was anxious to help other people, to worry about others, and to be thought of as something more than just a cancer survivor. She wanted to be a friend. One day a wife and mother. She wanted to be the person she used to be before her diagnosis. The same person, but better and stronger.

Chapter 26

The car's horn blared, frightening the horse.

From inside the buggy, Dorothy pulled on the reins as she tried to regain control. For four precarious seconds, the buggy wobbled, then righted itself, landing once again on all four wheels.

Dorothy responded by urging the horse to a trot.

By her side, Ella grabbed a hold of the bench in fright. "Dorothy, you must calm down," she pleaded. "Dorothy? Dorothy, do you understand?"

By her side, the other woman flinched. "I understand everything," she blurted.

"If you do, then you must listen." Seeking to ease the tension, Ella placed her fingers on Dorothy's arm. "Have a care, now. It's starting to rain and the roads are slick. You're going to injure your horse if you aren't more careful."

With a scowl, Dorothy yanked her arm away from Ella's grasp. "You're in no position to give me advice. You know nothing. Nothing!" And as if to prove Ella wrong, Dorothy snapped the reins to force the horse to move at an even faster clip. After a second's hesitation, the horse darted forward, its hooves clip-clopping loudly with each step.

The buggy jerked and swayed. The increased speed caused havoc with the elements, causing raindrops to fly inside the buggy's side opening. A breeze slapped against Ella's skirt and brushed against her cheeks. The nerves that had threatened to overwhelm her rose up, hard and triumphant. Tears she'd fought back pricked her eyelids. Her throat thickened, making it difficult to swallow.

There had been many times in her life when Ella had felt helpless. But never before had she been so afraid.

She'd never seen Dorothy like this—had never seen *anyone* act the way Dorothy was.

She was beyond angry, beyond any semblance of holding on to her control—or, it seemed, her sanity. Nothing Dorothy was saying was making sense; and she acted as if she had little care at all for their safety.

Not for the first time, Ella chided herself for even getting into the buggy. She should have trusted her instincts instead of listening to her heart. It was mighty obvious that any good feelings Dorothy had held for Ella were now long gone.

In fact, it was apparent that Dorothy was beyond focusing on anything but the delusions spinning in her head.

As another buggy approached, Ella frantically tried to see through the rain-splattered windshield. Maybe it was someone she recognized. Someone who could come to her aid. Unfortunately, the elderly man was unfamiliar.

Not wanting to give up, Ella still motioned to him. Perhaps she could make some kind of hand movement that would cause him to stop.

But before the man did anything more than peer at her strangely, Dorothy grabbed her fingers and squeezed hard. Unbearably hard. "Don't," she ordered.

Nervousness turned into sheer panic. "Dorothy, you had best slow down now," she shouted. "Better yet, you need to stop. You are behaving foolishly."

Slowly, Dorothy's head turned her way. "Foolishly?"

Seeing a flicker of recognition in her eyes, Ella nodded as she was finally able to pull her hand out of Dorothy's clinging grasp. "*Jah*. You are being terribly foolish. Dorothy, please, you must manage your temper. You are going to cause an accident. We could get hurt!"

"I will not get hurt. I'm in control, Ella," she whispered, not even bothering to look Ella's way. Almost triumphantly, she added, "Do you understand now? Finally? You cannot win. Only I will win."

Ella bit her bottom lip as her heart slammed into her chest. Any hope for encouraging reason was fading—as was the foolish wish for a peaceful end to the ride. The rain came at them harder, soaking their bonnets, coating Ella's glasses.

Once again, she pulled them off and wiped the lenses with the inside of one of her sleeves.

But when she put the glasses on again, Ella almost wished her vision was still distorted. Now she could see Dorothy's knuckles turn white and the tendons in her neck turn sharp. It was becoming more obvious that Dorothy was anything but in control. The buggy was sliding off the road with every curve.

She could barely control the vehicle.

Once again, Ella berated herself for ever accepting the ride.

After speaking with Loyal and Ms. Donovan she'd been walking back to her apartment, going over in her mind the best way to address her concerns to Dorothy, when Dorothy herself had pulled up beside her.

"There's no need for you to walk, it's starting to rain," she'd said. Her expression had been sweet; her voice kind and melodic.

And because her new pale blue dress was already becoming dotted with raindrops, Ella had taken her up on the offer. They were only four blocks from their duplex—not so far of a distance to sit together awkwardly, and just far enough to be glad she was out of the rain.

Never had Ella imagined Dorothy's offer had only been a ploy to get her into the buggy.

When Dorothy had passed their duplex, then turned onto a near-vacant side street, Ella had been confused. That feeling had soon grown into panic, then true fear.

Now she was holding on for dear life. Now she was at Dorothy's mercy.

As a car passed, the vehicle's tires shot up flecks of water. The splashes spurted up the side of the buggy and inside, soaking them and straining Ella's already frayed nerves. The horse neighed its displeasure.

Now Dorothy's buggy was practically flying down the road . . . on the way to the country, away from Jacob's Crossing and everything that Ella knew.

With each passing yard, Ella's worries grew—and with it, a sense of desperation overtook her.

And still the questions multiplied and scrambled in her head. "Dorothy, where are we going?"

"Away."

"Away? Away where?"

"Some place quiet. Some place where we can talk."

"But we could have talked back at the house."

"Oh, *nee,* Ella. Never will you go back there. That is my home. It's not yours any longer."

The hair raised on Ella's arms. She was more afraid than she could ever remember being.

But with that fear came the knowledge that she was willing to fight, to do whatever it took to survive this ordeal. To convince Dorothy to let her leave.

With that in mind, she kept her voice as calm as she could. "We can talk right now. What has upset you so much?"

Dorothy glanced her way, pure scorn illuminating her eyes. "What has upset me?" she repeated. "Everything that you've done. You've taken me for granted, Ella."

"I certainly haven't . . ."

"You've taken me for granted," she repeated. "You used me, and what's worse, you don't even care. I was the one who visited you when you were alone at your farm." Her voice turned harsher. "Do you even remember how you were feeling when your mother lay in her bed, dying?"

Each word felt like a sharp stab. "Of course I remember how I was feeling." She'd been in a tunnel of darkness. Everything in her life had felt gray and full of despair. "And of course I remember your visits."

"You should. No one else visited," she added, her voice full of derision. "No one else cared, Ella."

"That is not true. People came." She wasn't going to let Dorothy turn the already horrible time into something worse.

"People came to see your mother, Ella. Not you. They were never there for you. You were alone. Forgotten."

Forgotten. That had, indeed, been how she'd felt. Everyone else had moved on, while she'd stayed behind, doing what was right. Making her mother as comfortable as possible, doing her best to take care of their home and farm.

But then, of course, she'd failed at every turn. Her mother still had been in pain and ultimately passed on.

And the farm had been too much—and too expensive for her to keep.

Even Loyal's exuberance to share with her the renovations couldn't hide the vague niggling feeling that she'd failed to keep up the house as well.

And though Corrine and Mattie and other people from their community had stopped by, their visits weren't with any sort of regularity. Often, they were explained as an afterthought.

Was Dorothy right?

Dorothy laughed. "Now you know what I mean, don't you? Nobody missed you, Ella. Everyone was too intent on their own life and their own problems to pay any attention to yours." She darted another look Ella's way. "Everyone except for me."

Dorothy's hurtful words did, indeed, strike a nerve. Living on the farm, with only her mother who had been near death . . . it had been a horribly isolating experience. Many nights she had gone to sleep, sure that no one had been thinking of her. And if they did, it wasn't more than a passing concern.

And as she'd held her dear mother's hand on her last day on earth, Ella finally allowed herself to contemplate the terrible truth—perhaps no one ever would care about her.

Against her best efforts, old hurts rushed forward. In a blink, all the confidence she'd felt growing inside of her started to wither.

Outside, the clouds darkened as twilight approached and the storm intensified. Raindrops splattered on the pavement, causing puffs of steam to appear.

Water had now soaked through most of her dress. Her arms and legs were wet. Little by little, the fabric got heavier, feeling tighter and even more confining.

They rounded a curve. Dorothy's horse slowed for a brief instant before picking up speed.

In spite of her efforts to remain strong, Ella started to cry. Her tears mixed with the raindrops on her face. Together, they trickled down her cheeks and fell onto her lap.

Perhaps Dorothy really was the winner.

Ella knew she'd never felt more lost.

As if she sensed victory, Dorothy's posture changed and her voice turned triumphant. "I was all you had. And when it was just me, you acted as if you cared about me."

"Of course I cared. I still do care."

"No. You were only using me to get what you wanted. In spite of all my efforts, in spite of everything I've done for you, you forgot me, Ella."

"No—"

"You've forgotten me. I know you so well; I know what you were thinking. You were going to leave me for Loyal. No matter what it took or what you had to do, you were going to catch him."

"It wasn't like that. It isn't like that."

But Dorothy wasn't listening. Peering straight ahead, she lowered her voice. "I had to stop you. I had to stop you from abandoning me. Again."

Again?

"Dorothy, I live next to you. We were working together."

"But everything isn't right between us. You're too different, Ella . . ."

"I'm the same I've always been."

Dorothy shook her head. "No. You're turning into the worst sort of woman. You're pretending to be something you're not. All to gain Loyal Weaver's attention."

Ella blinked. For a moment, she let the harsh, difficult words sink in; and for a split second, she believed them. Then she realized that Loyal wasn't that kind of man.

He wasn't the kind of man who flirted

without true intentions. He wasn't the kind of person who kissed without thoughts and care behind it.

And she wasn't the kind of woman who did that, either.

Gathering her courage, Ella said, "Let me have the reins."

"Of course not."

"Dorothy, I'm not going to sit here and let you do this."

"There's nothing you can do. There's nothing at all you can ever do. I won." She looked at Ella and smiled.

Ella realized that Dorothy had gone completely off balance. There would be no reasoning with her. There would be nothing to do except try to escape.

Lord, please help me, she prayed. *I know I've asked you for so much, but I need you more than ever. I can't fight her alone.*

The horse neighed and jostled.

A car attempting to pass them screeched as a truck approaching them laid on its horn.

Scaring the horse. The buggy shook. Bumped. With a hard thump it righted itself, but then jumped and swayed again. Ella gripped the seat. Grabbed at the opening, hoping there was some way she could will the careening buggy to rights.

Dorothy started. Yelled.

As the buggy bolted off the road, breaking away from the horse, tethers snapped. Ella's grip slipped.

The buggy crashed to the side.

Car tires screeched. The horse cried out.

So did Ella as she watched Dorothy fall. She had only a second's glimpse as the woman landed on the hard pavement and slid to the side.

Then she gasped as the buggy fell on her.

Her lungs screaming, Ella heaved. With a last bit of effort, she strained to get free.

But it was no use. She was trapped hard against the wet ground.

"Please!" she called out. Hoping that someone would hear her.

That someone would save her.

But all she felt was the cold stinging needles of sharp raindrops as her world turned black.

Chapter 27

Frantic, Mattie pounded on the front door of John Weaver's shop for a second time. "John?" she called out, almost oblivious to the crash of thunder and lightning above her head. "Mr. Weaver?"

When no sound of rushing footsteps greeted her, she pounded again. Harder. "Oh, please, please answer me," she said, though she wasn't sure if she was speaking to John or the Lord.

The fact was, she needed some help, and she needed it as soon as possible.

After waiting for the space of a few breaths, Mattie knocked her knuckles

against the hard oak one more time, desperately hoping Graham and Calvin's uncle
would suddenly appear.

In the back of her mind, she prayed for
another plan to appear in her mind. Quickly.
No matter what, she needed to locate Ella.

Even if she couldn't find another person
to help, she had to figure out some way to
come to her friend's aid. Even if all she
could offer was moral support.

Just when she'd been on the verge of
turning around, the door to The Kaffi Haus
flew open and John appeared.

For a full second, they stood staring at
each other. Mattie gazing at him in wonder, wondering if he was, indeed, the answer to her prayers. John looking frightened
to death.

Looking her up and down, he gasped,
"Mattie, what is it?"

"I need your help," she blurted.

When his eyebrows rose, she tried to
calm herself enough. Trying again, she
said, "I need your help, John. Please. I'm
sorry, but I don't know who else to turn to."

With a worried frown, John stepped out,
circled one comforting arm around her
shoulder and guided her inside. Out of the

rain. With a kick, the door closed behind him. "What's wrong, Mattie?" he asked gently, just as if he feared she was about to fall apart. "Are you ill again? Do you need to go to the hospital?"

Turning to face him, she shook her head. "*Nee*. The problem—it's not about me."

"Then what?"

"It's Ella."

He blinked, obviously trying to place the girl's name. "Loyal's Ella?"

She nodded. "John, please help Loyal and me find her." When he continued to stare at her blankly, she rushed to try to explain. "John, I think something awful has happened to her."

Though his body tensed, he still seemed far too calm.

"Mattie, what in the world are you talking about?" He glanced at the rain pelting the windows. "Is she caught out in the storm?"

"Most likely. But John, that isn't the problem! I think Dorothy Zook got mad at her."

"And who is Dorothy?"

"Her friend. Well, she used to be her friend. But now I don't think she's that at all. In fact, I think Dorothy has maybe hurt Ella. Or worse," she added, voicing her deepest concerns. "Oh, but I'm terribly worried, John. We need to go find her. Offer our protection." Grabbing hold of his arm, she said, "Actually, I think maybe we should even call the police."

To her dismay, John's shoulders relaxed. He even looked to be fighting off a smile. "Oh, Mattie, it's just the storm that's got you upset. Don't worry yourself so much, I'm sure Ella will be just fine."

She shook her head and opened her mouth to tell him that she wasn't afraid of a rainstorm—when John continued talking again, his voice now slick and even. As smooth as syrup.

"I know the thunder is bad, but I promise, it's just rain. Hey, how about a fresh cup of coffee? It will warm you up." He nodded as he walked toward the coffeemaker. "Yes. You can rest here for a bit and then I'll drive you home."

Pure frustration made her raise her voice as she followed him to the sink. "*Nee!* No, John Weaver! My fears have nothing to do with me or my health. You need to hear me, to listen to what I am sayin'."

Adrenaline made her dig her fingers into his forearm, stopping him from pulling out a coffee filter. "I know what I'm saying sounds fanciful, but I wouldn't be here if I didn't need you." When he finally froze, she moved her hand to his. Reaching out, she curved her hand around his own and softly squeezed. "Please, don't laugh me off. I need your help."

A whole new look entered his eyes. "Okay. I hear you. And I'm finally listening. What's going on?"

Taking a deep breath, she said, "After I saw you, I went down to the library. I thought I'd visit with Ella."

A flash of awareness entered his eyes before he blinked it away. "And?"

"When I got there, instead of seeing Ella, I saw Loyal and Katie and Ms. Donovan." She paused to explain. "All were upset. It turns out that Ella had told Loyal she was going to confront Dorothy this afternoon. She wanted to put a stop to the awful rumors Dorothy had told Ms. Donovan about her."

"Okay . . ."

"After talking, Loyal and I left to make sure everything was all right. Because of Dorothy's actions of late, we felt that Ella might have been in over her head. But when we got to her house, we guessed that Dorothy picked Ella up in her buggy."

"Where's Loyal?"

"He went back to the library to collect Katie."

He pursed his lips. "I know you're worried, but sometimes it's better to think the best instead of the worst. Maybe they're patching things up?"

"If they are, and Loyal and I are making fools of ourselves, I'll be mighty relieved. But, John, I don't think I'm mistaken about this." Lowering her voice, she said, "I've had almost a year of sitting by myself and thinking about life and death. I've watched people and tried to gauge their actions. I don't have a good feeling about this."

John looked at her for a long moment before finally nodding. "All right, then. Let me lock up the shop. We'll go to the library, get Loyal and Katie, and go find Ella."

Impulsively, she hugged him. "Oh, *Danke*."

"It's nothing," he murmured right back in Pennsylvania Dutch, making her realize that he wasn't far removed from their lives after all.

"Would you like to run by the Weaver's farm and get Graham, too?"

Feeling her cheeks heat, she turned away, hoping John wouldn't notice. "There's no need for him to get involved. He's, uh, seeing Jenna now."

"All right. If you're sure?"

"I'm positive. This isn't about me, John. I'm really worried."

"If you're worried, I am too. Let's go."

Within two minutes, John had locked up the store and was helping her into his truck. Then he pulled out, turned right, and sped the few blocks to the library.

As soon as he stopped, Loyal and Katie joined them. "Where do you want to go first, Loyal?" John asked.

"Let's go to the farm first," he said. "Perhaps Dorothy was just giving Ella a ride over there."

Mattie shook her head. "But—"

"Let's not borrow trouble, Mattie. Enough trouble follows us, I promise you that."

As the truck sped along the highway, Mattie finally allowed herself to close her eyes and pray. She gave thanks that John was in their lives. They needed the speed his truck could give them.

She gave thanks for friends that both she and Ella could lean on. And, surpris-

ing herself, she gave thanks for her cancer. Now she realized that if she hadn't
suffered, if she hadn't spent so much time
alone, watching people, thinking about
other's problems and dreams, she wouldn't
have felt so sure that Ella needed her
now.

I know I haven't believed in you, she silently prayed. *I know I thought you'd left
me. But now I realize you'd been there all
along, helping me through. And helping
me grow up. Helping me see that there's
more to the world than I had ever realized.*
**Reminding me that I'd once taken so
much for granted. Please be with Ella
right now. Please be with all of us.**

As they waited at a stoplight, Loyal
looked her way. "Are you okay?"

"Yes. I . . . I was just praying," she murmured, half afraid he would think she was
being even sillier than he'd first thought.

But instead of smiling, he merely nodded. "I think that's a very good idea. If
what you suspect is true—if Ella really is
in terrible danger—we're going to need
everyone's help. Especially our Lord's."

Mattie forced herself to breathe slowly
as the light turned green and he drove with

the traffic flow. Never had it felt like it had taken so long to get to the Weaver farm.

As Mattie sat beside him praying, Loyal added his own prayers, too. *Please be with Ella, Lord,* he silently asked. *Please help her, and please let her know that she isn't alone. She has You protecting her, and all of us on her side as well.*

When they reached the farm, Loyal helped Katie out of the truck. Calvin met them at the door. Obviously seeing their worried expressions, he looked from one to the other. "What's going on?"

Briefly Mattie filled Calvin in on what she'd heard at the library and how they think they figured out that Dorothy had Ella in her buggy. After a quick hug, they left the Weaver farm and headed toward Ella's old farm. Loyal's new one.

"I'm plenty worried, Loyal," Mattie said after a bit. "I keep feeling like Ella is in danger. I don't want to be right, but what if I am?"

Loyal eyed Mattie, then looked over her head and shared an exchange with his uncle. What Mattie was saying sounded completely off the wall, but for some reason he didn't doubt her words.

Snippets of his past conversations with Ella came flashing back. He recalled every comment she'd shared with him about Dorothy, and how concerned and confused she'd felt about her longtime friend.

Then Loyal remembered discussing Dorothy with his mother. Recalled how his *mamm* had said Dorothy felt like everyone she'd loved abandoned her. That it had made her feel helpless and angry.

It really all did make sense.

Just as John was about to turn into the entrance to the farm, his uncle's cell phone rang.

After checking the incoming call's phone number, John took the call. "Jayne?" he said, his voice soft. "What's going on?"

But then John's curious expression turned to a scowl as he listened. "When? Are you sure? Where? Okay. Yes. Yes."

Mattie met Loyal's gaze and frowned.

Finally, John hung up.

Running a hand through his hair, he turned to both of them. "Um . . . that was Jayne. One of the patrons just came running into the library to tell Jayne about an accident she saw. It . . . it was a buggy accident."

Mattie paled. "Are you sure?"

"She thinks so. Mattie, Loyal . . . Jayne said she heard the accident was a bad one. Two women were involved. She fears it was Dorothy and Ella."

Loyal shook his head, every bit of him wanting to deny everything John was telling him.

Surely this couldn't be happening. Surely Jayne misunderstood. Got the details wrong.

But what if she was right? What if he lost Ella now, just when he was realizing how important she was to him?

"Can we go to where it was?" Mattie asked, her voice hoarse.

John blinked. "Of course. Let's go."

As the truck raced down the highway, Loyal noticed Mattie was shaking. "Are you all right?"

Turning her head, she looked at him and frowned. "*Nee,* I don't think I am," she said slowly. "All of a sudden I'm realizing that I've taken so many things for granted, Loyal. And worse . . . I think I took Ella for granted."

She bit her lip. "Why didn't I spend more time with her? I knew her mother had just passed on. I knew it hurt her to lose her farm. But instead of being there for her, I stayed in my own little world, scared that my cancer was returning."

John stayed silent as he continued to speed down the highway, but Loyal couldn't help commenting on what Mattie said. "I feel the same way. She's lived next to us for as long as I can remember, but I never reached out to her. I thought she was boring. Not exciting. All last year, I'm afraid I was just hoping for her to put the farm up for auction. If you took her for granted . . . what kind of person am I? Surely the very worst sort."

"I feel so guilty," Mattie said.

John braked as the street curved, then gradually his speed increased as he passed a white sedan. "I hate to disrupt your pity party," he said, "but I think you're both being too hard on yourselves."

"I don't think so," Loyal said, slightly stung by his uncle's attitude.

"First of all, no one would have guessed that Dorothy would actually harm Ella. From what you've both said, for years Dorothy's been her friend, yes?"

Mattie nodded, "That is true."

"Now, next, there's something to be said for that old saying about hindsight being twenty-twenty. It's easy to look back and wish for things to be different. Or that you would have acted in a different way." He swallowed as he turned right, then accelerated on the near-empty road. "I know I have many regrets about the things I've done. However, you both are forgetting something very important."

"And what is that?" Loyal asked.

"None of us has been walking through life alone. God is with us, even when we aren't holding out our hands to Him."

"You really think that?" Mattie asked.

"I do. I think our Lord has been with me, even when I make mistakes." He laughed dryly. "Maybe even *especially* when I make mistakes. Sometimes people think of Christians as people who try to be better than everyone else. Or people who don't think they are as fallible as everyone else. But I think it's just the opposite. I think Christians know they mess up and say things they shouldn't, and can admit they hadn't done things they wish they had."

Understanding dawned. "Because we aren't looking for perfection," Loyal murmured. "We're simply looking for a place to belong."

John slowed the truck as flashing lights appeared in the distance. "That is right," he said softly as the muscles in his cheek tensed. "All of us just want a place to live and to be happy, and to know that we're accepted. And if we can get that—well, that should be enough for anyone, I'm thinking."

John's words sunk in as they slowly approached a grouping of police cars, a fire truck, and an ambulance.

And just as John was pulling the truck off the side of the road, Loyal spotted a mare. She was cut and bleeding but was on her feet. A good sign.

However, the buggy was on its side.

Mattie gasped. "That's Dorothy's horse. I'm sure of it." The moment John pulled the keys out of the ignition, she unbuckled and unlocked her door.

"Patience, Mattie," Loyal said, stopping her quick exit with a staying hand. "All we'll get for running into the mass of vehicles is to be asked to leave."

"I'm calm. But we need to get over there soon," she said as she got out of the truck.

After all three of them had exited, they

walked on the grassy shoulder toward the accident site. Loyal's heart was beating so fast, he was sure both John and Mattie could hear it.

When they were at about five hundred feet away, a police officer approached them. "Stop."

Loyal took a breath. "But—"

"No excuses. We've got enough going on here without people stopping to look. You all need to move along, folks."

"But I think we know the woman in the accident," Mattie said. "There were women in the buggy, yes?"

The policeman's expression turned to one of compassion. "I'm sorry."

Mattie blanched. "Why? What happened? Where are they?"

Loyal gripped her arm as tears started falling down her cheeks. Doing his best to remain composed, he swallowed hard. "Can . . . May we see them?"

The policeman's cheeks reddened. "No. I'm sorry . . ."

John stepped forward. "Where are they?" Pointing to an ambulance he said, "Are they in there?"

"One is. But we're waiting on the coroner."

Loyal didn't understand. "Who is that?"

"One woman is already on her way to the hospital. And one . . . I'm sorry to tell you, didn't make it."

Loyal wrapped an arm around Mattie when she swayed. "Can you tell us who is on the way to the hospital?"

"I'm sorry, sir, but we must notify her family first."

"But Ella doesn't have any family," Mattie said.

Loyal straightened his shoulders. "That's not quite right. She has me," he said, realizing he meant it with his whole heart. No longer would she be alone. If God would grant them another chance, he was going to ask her to marry him. To be his forever.

But he couldn't do that until he knew the truth. Steeling himself for the worst but hoping for the best, he stepped forward. Alone.

Then he asked the question that had been burning in all their minds. "Officer, please tell me the truth. Is Ella Hostetler on her way to the hospital? Or did she die here today?"

Chapter 28

The first thing Ella noticed when she awakened was a tube attached to the top of her hand. Raising her hand close, she could see that clear tape fastened the tube securely. It looked scary and like it should sting as the medicine in the tube filled her veins, drop by drop.

But, amazingly, it didn't.

However, every other part of body ached something terrible. She felt as if every bone and muscle had been jarred, pushed, and bruised. Even her head pounded. After wiggling her toes and stretching her fingers, she carefully patted her forehead. There she discovered a wide bandage across her hairline. With a wince, she put her hand down.

And then discovered that her leg was impossible to move.

Her eyes tried to focus, but of course without her glasses nothing could be discerned. All she was aware of was a tingly antiseptic smell and how comfortably warm the room felt.

Oh, but she'd been so cold and wet.

Where am I?

"Ah, you decided to join us after all," a woman suddenly said, her tone as bright as a brand-new day. She stood up from the chair she occupied and stepped close. Two cool, soft hands cupped Ella's. "We were starting to get worried about you."

Ella shifted, trying to see where exactly she was. But she didn't have her glasses on, and everything was only a blur.

"Easy now," the nurse murmured. "You're in the hospital." She paused. "Do you understand? You were in an accident. A buggy accident. An ambulance brought you here."

Ah, yes. She'd been in an *accident*.

Ella gripped the metal bar on the side of

her bed to steady herself as waves of pain mixed with flashes of memories. Now she remembered holding on for dear life while the buggy fell.

She recalled the horse screaming.

She remembered crying and calling for help as the rain soaked her skin. Of feeling completely alone in the world.

She looked at the nurse again, this time squinting her eyes in an attempt to see her better. Oh, she hated her poor vision. It gave her the worst sort of disadvantage—made her feel completely dependent on other people.

And so helpless. Like she was at everyone else's mercy. "Glasses?" she muttered. Her mouth felt like cotton, and her brain didn't seem to be working properly. But getting back her sight would be so wonderfully good.

"Glasses? Oh! That, I can help you with, believe it or not." Slowly, the nurse slipped Ella's frames on her face.

Ella blinked as her eyes became accustomed to the lenses. Right away, she saw that the room was painted a pale green and that the nurse was wearing a pink shirt and pants—and that the shirt had polka dots printed on it. The nurse had freckles and brown frizzy hair. And a beautiful, toothy smile. *"Danke,"* she murmured.

Looking at Ella's eyes, the nurse said, "The EMT set these on your gurney—no one could believe that the glasses didn't shatter." The nurse's grin widened as she tilted her head and looked at Ella proudly. "And with lenses like these, we knew you would certainly need them."

Ella blinked again and took more notice of the room. There was a curtain hanging on one side, and lots of portable-looking cabinets. A few bottles and cups were sitting on a table; and across from where Ella was lying, there was a television hooked up to the wall.

Ella looked again at the woman. She was still smiling, but now her eyes held a new hint of worry. Like there was something on the tip of her tongue. As if there was much more that she wasn't saying.

Which created a panic in Ella. "What happened?" she asked, trying to sit up. But the nurse gently put a hand on her shoulder to hold her safely in place.

"Don't move so quickly, dear. I think it would be best for everyone if you took it easy. Your poor body has been through a lot, you know."

As Ella tried to process the words through her foggy brain, she felt a whole new rush of panic. "Horse . . . ?" she sputtered as more memories of the buggy accident crashed forward.

The nurse shook her head. "I'm afraid I don't know the answer about that. We've been busy trying to patch you up. You've got a good bump on your forehead, a broken leg, a fractured collarbone, and stitches in three or four places."

Ella sighed. Well that explained her bandage and her leg. "Hurt. I hurt," she murmured.

"I know. I'm going to give you some medicine for the pain." She stood up. "But first I need to let the doctor know you're awake. And he's going to want to see you."

"All right," she mumbled, though she didn't really know why she did. It wasn't like she had a say in how things went.

The nurse turned away, then turned back to her, her fluffy hair swinging with the motion. "Ella, I'm also going to ask if you can see your visitors." Eyes shining, she said,

"It would be a shame to make everyone wait much longer to say hello."

"What?"

"Your fiancé is out there," she said with a smile. "Why, he's practically worn a hole in the carpet, pacing back and forth like he has."

She left before Ella could clarify things. To tell her that she had no fiancé. And that she surely didn't have all that many people who would come all the way to the hospital to see her.

Leaning back against the very hard pillow, she tried to review everything the nurse had told her. But nothing made sense.

Why had she only spoken about the accident in the vaguest of terms? Did she really not know anything? And what about Dorothy?

Her head started to pound worse. She closed her eyes, seeking relief. But none came. With each second her pain intensified and her confusion grew. Slowly, she inhaled and exhaled, hoping the slow and steady breathing would help alleviate some of her confusion, and maybe the worst of the pain.

Breathe in. Out. Don't think. *Don't* guess. *Don't* try to understand.

"Ella?" A hand touched her forehead. Her arm. "Ella? Can you hear me? I hope you didn't fall asleep on me again. Wake up."

Slowly, she opened her eyes. With a start, she realized she'd fallen asleep with her glasses on. "Oh," she gasped.

There was a youngish-looking man in a pair of green scrubs and a stethoscope around his neck. He smiled when she met his gaze.

"Hi. There you are. I'm Dr. Roberts." He paused. "Do you understand that you're in the hospital?"

Ella nodded.

"Good. Beverly told me you are stiff and sore, hmm? And in a lot of pain?"

"*Jah*. I mean, yes."

"Well, that's to be expected." He held up her wrist and took her pulse. After a moment, he murmured something to the nurse on his left. Next, he removed her glasses, looked in her eyes with a bright light, then gently set them back on her nose. "You're pretty beat up, Ella; and I'm afraid this is one of those times when you're going to feel worse before you feel better. But hang in there. Beverly's going to give you some medicine through your IV to help make you more comfortable."

He paused and patted her forearm gently. "Now, the good news is that the break in your leg was a clean one, and can be set as soon as the swelling goes down. As far as your fractured collarbone, we're just going to keep you bandaged. Understand?"

Ella nodded.

"Very good. So, if all goes well, you might even get out of here in two days."

Two days? The idea of staying in this strange place was upsetting, but she supposed it couldn't be helped. "That's fine," she murmured, supposing some response was expected.

"All right. I'll come back in a while. But for the time being, I think we'll go ahead and let your man in here. And your friends, of course. They seem like a real nice bunch."

Ella stared at him, stunned. *Man?*

His eyes narrowed. "Ella, are you all right? Do you have any questions?"

She had too many to count. So all she did was shake her head and hope that

sometime in the future she'd be able to
think again.

The doctor grinned. "I'll be back in a few
hours." As he passed the nurse on his way
out, he said, "Beverly, keep the visit to a
minimum, would you?"

Ella hardly heard Beverly's response
because in walked Loyal. And Mattie.
And Graham, and Corrine and her husband. Even Jayne Donovan was there.
And Loyal's Uncle John!

Oh, but there were so many people, especially for a woman who had been feeling like she was virtually alone in the world
just a few short months ago.

Ella was so overcome, she merely
stared at them all in wonder.

Loyal got to her side first. Ella watched
him approach, his expression stern and
serious, and completely centered on her.
Her gaze skittered around the room. Graham's eyebrows rose as he watched Loyal.
Mattie looked smug.

John and Jayne were both smiling, yet
also looked ill at ease standing next to each
other.

Then Ella had eyes for no one but Loyal—
and he seemed incapable of doing any-

thing but looking at her intently. She felt him examine every single nick and scratch and bandage.

"Oh, Ella," he murmured, his voice so soft, like a caress. "Look at you. We've been so terribly worried about you."

That caring tone of voice was all she needed for the tears to flow. Frustrated, she blinked them away.

"What a state you're in," he murmured, leaning close and carefully wiping the tears with a gentle touch. Next he took her hand and folded both of his around it. Right there, in front of everyone!

Quickly, Ella looked toward Corrine. But Corrine simply smiled.

With effort, she tried to reply. "That's what usually happens when a person is in a buggy accident."

His expression softened, his eyes looking languid—almost as if they were about to tear up. "We're so glad nothing worse happened to you." He looked toward John. "Things were pretty scary, weren't they?"

John nodded. "Ella, I hope I never see another buggy accident like that as long as I live."

"My heart was in my throat," Mattie said.

Ella felt her world spinning. Not a bit of what they were saying felt right. She'd been alone with Dorothy. How had John seen the accident?

And furthermore, how did everyone even know she'd been taken to the hospital?

And why was Loyal now acting as if she was his sweetheart? "Loyal, why are you here?"

"That has to be the silliest question you've ever asked me, Ella Hostetler."

She couldn't help it. Little by little, her lips curved upward, even though the cuts on her face hurt and it was an effort to do most anything. "Why?" she asked again.

"Because I couldn't stay away."

His words embarrassed her. Seemed like they were too much. But oh, how she did enjoy hearing them! Suddenly too shy to stare at him, she moved her gaze beyond. "Mattie, Corrine, John, Jayne, Graham—thank you all for coming."

Graham stepped forward. "I shouldn't ask how you're doing because it's fairly obvious. But . . . how are you?"

Loyal almost pushed his brother away, but Ella took the question seriously. "I'm alive," she finally said. "And for that, I am grateful."

Mattie slipped in between them both. "I was so scared, Ella, when we were driving with John trying to find you. I thought my pulse was going to go crazy! I worried we wouldn't find you in time."

"In time?"

Loyal shook his head as he carefully clasped her hand in his. "That's nothing we need to think about now," he said. "All we need to think about now is how we can make you feel better." He held up a cup. "Would you like some water?"

She nodded, but knew that she didn't want to be shielded from the truth. "Please tell me the truth. What happened?"

"Mattie's the one who got us all looking for you," Jayne explained. "And John Weaver drove Loyal and Mattie around in his truck."

"As soon as I discovered that you had left in Dorothy's buggy," explained Mattie, "I just didn't feel right. I didn't trust her."

Finally someone had mentioned Dorothy!

"Mattie was sure that Dorothy had taken you against your will," Loyal said. "Was that true?"

"Jah." The details were fuzzy, but little by little snippets of the storm and the ride and Dorothy's words all came tumbling back. "The police asked me questions when I got into the ambulance," Ella blurted, suddenly remembering all the flashing lights, sirens, the men who moved the buggy, and the other men who put her on the stretcher.

More details flashed forward, but in no kind of order. She remembered the man identifying himself as a police detective and his questions. "Why do you think the police are involved?" Worry spiraled as her friends exchanged glances.

Ella watched Loyal glare at Mattie, then look at John for guidance. Slowly John nodded in his direction.

"Loyal, please tell me what you know," she begged. "I really do want to know the truth."

Loyal pressed his other hand over her palm. "Well . . . do you remember Dorothy picking you up when you came home from work?"

Ella started to nod, but it hurt too much, so she spoke. "Yes." Remembering Ms. Donovan was in the room, she looked at her hands. "I quit."

Jayne tsked. "Ella, you should have never quit. I want you to work for me for years."

Though the motion hurt, Ella lifted her chin and looked Jayne's way. "But Dorothy said that you were mad . . ."

"Dorothy lied," she retorted.

Loyal leaned forward, claiming her attention with his caring gaze. "So . . . Dorothy found you when you were walking?"

"*Jah*. She looked embarrassed. She asked if I'd like a ride home."

"And you went."

"I thought she meant what she said. I thought she was going to apologize. But she didn't." She closed her eyes as more memories of that scary, horrible ride came floating back.

"Instead, she started driving the buggy away from town?" Loyal murmured.

"Yes. And she said all kinds of terrible things. Dorothy told me that I was a terrible person. And then she started driving faster and faster." It all came back to her as she remembered the rain and the wind and the feeling of complete helplessness.

Like she was completely at Dorothy's mercy. Like she was completely alone.

She'd figured no one else would have known where they were. And no one would ever find them.

And though she'd prayed to God to help her, He hadn't seemed to be listening.

"Ella? Can you tell us what happened next?"

"I'll try. She kept driving that poor horse faster—and I kept asking her to slow down. And then a car tried to pass us, but another one was coming, and everyone veered to go out of the way." Things were fuzzy then. "I just remember falling, and the buggy falling on top of me."

Loyal cleared his throat. "That's what we heard, Ella. That you have survived a whole buggy falling on you."

Mattie smiled broadly. "I'm so glad you're going to be okay. I'm going to nurse you! You can stay at my house. It will be wonderful-*gut*."

Oh, she was getting so tired. Her lids were feeling heavy. With effort, Ella did her best to concentrate. "I . . . I thank you. Because I need to find some place to stay now. Dorothy kicked me out."

All the people around her exchanged

glances. The tension in the room rose. Graham murmured, "Loyal?"

"What?" Ella said. "What are you all not saying?" Suddenly, it came to her. So far, no one had mentioned how Dorothy was doing. Not the police, not the doctors and nurses, not even her friends. "Where is Dorothy? Is she in the hospital, too?"

Loyal shook his head.

Ella couldn't have been more confused. "She didn't get hurt? I could have sworn she flew out of the buggy before I did." Desperately, she tried to recall that short span of seconds. But all she could really remember was Dorothy not being there when the buggy fell on top of her. "Did she really only get a few cuts and bruises?"

Mattie pushed her way to Loyal's side and gently smoothed her hair back from her face. "It was worse than that."

Loyal sighed. "There's no easy way to say this. Dorothy, she died, Ella. Dorothy died in the buggy accident."

She was stunned. And scared because she didn't know how she felt about that.

She knew she should feel grief, but she

felt relief that she had survived, too. Relief and sadness and confusion.

And right behind it, guilt. Of course she shouldn't feel anything but sorrow. Closing her eyes, she turned away from her friends and tried to collect herself.

But instead of leaving her to deal with the shock by herself, Mattie edged closer and gently wrapped her arms around her. "It's okay, Ella," she whispered.

"*Nee*. It is not."

"I understand. But please know . . . whatever happened was meant to happen. I promise! It was God's will."

Mattie had such conviction in her voice, Ella looked at her with wonder. "You truly think so?"

"It's all I do know," Mattie said, her expression sober. "God is with us, always. Even when we're not with him. I'm proof of that."

Ella clung to those words long into the night. Even after the nurses said good night and the sky darkened.

Even after she'd said her prayers and waited for some kind of peace to claim her.

Chapter 29

John followed Jayne out to the parking lot while everyone else made plans and talked with the nurses.

"Jayne? Do you have a minute?" he called out.

She turned abruptly. "Of course." Looking concerned, she said, "Is something wrong?"

"No. Well, nothing else with Ella," he corrected. "I just wanted to talk to you for a minute. I, um, I didn't think we resolved everything between us."

The eyes he was so taken with widened, then blinked. When she focused on him again, her expression looked carefully blank. "There wasn't anything to resolve. All we had was just a date."

He knew it had been more. There had been a real connection between them. He'd felt their tension, felt the awareness. Though he was clumsy around women, even he had known that she would have accepted if he'd asked her out again.

"The night when I came over for steaks—it was one of the nicest evenings I've had for some time."

"I enjoyed myself, too."

She gazed at him, waiting. And he knew she wasn't going to let him off anymore. If he was going to stop her in the parking lot, she wanted an explanation. "When I left, I planned to ask you out again."

"But you didn't even call."

His rudeness embarrassed him, and reminded him, too, of how different small-town life was than in the middle of the city. Here, you couldn't avoid people by slinking into the shadows of crowds.

"I didn't call because I realized that while I liked you, I also liked another woman."

She narrowed her eyes. "Well. I guess I

understand." With a pivot of her heel, she turned away.

John rushed to her side. "I'm not explaining this well. At all. Listen, Jayne, it was like this. When I moved here, I met two women. You and Mary."

"Mary."

"You are who I thought I should spend my time with. I mean, Jayne, you're the type of woman I used to dream of dating."

The way she was looking at him, like she was trying her best not to roll her eyes, made him feel like a jerk.

He rushed on before he made an even greater fool of himself than he already was. "But I also liked visiting with Mary, too."

"Wasn't she special too, John?" Her voice was more than a bit sarcastic.

"She's Amish."

All the scorn in her gaze vanished in a heartbeat. "Really?"

"Mary's Amish and is a widow and has a son. In short, she's everything I shouldn't want. I left the order. I don't know much about raising kids. But every time I was near her, I found myself wanting to go back to my roots."

"For her?"

He nodded. "And for myself." While she looked at him, so untrusting, so skeptical, John forced himself to try to explain. "Jayne, I don't know if you can ever forgive me, but please understand that this is why I didn't call. It's a poor excuse, but it's the truth. I didn't call you because all this time, I haven't been sure about what to do."

"What did she say when you told her how you were feeling?"

"I haven't said a thing to her. I've just been waiting and hoping that the right words would come to me." He looked back at the front of the hospital. "But Ella's accident has made me realize that it's wrong to keep waiting for the perfect time."

"You know what? You're right. You should go talk to Mary."

"I hope one day you'll forgive me."

Her eyes sparkled. "John, I don't expect to fall in love every time I cook a man dinner. I've only been upset with the way you handled things. I didn't know what I did wrong."

Instinctively, John knew she was more hurt than that. He knew she'd been expecting him to call, expecting them to go out again soon.

After all, he'd certainly insinuated that he would.

"You didn't do a thing wrong," he said. Realizing even as he said the words out loud that they were insignificant.

Pulling her keys out of her purse, Jayne looked at him closely. "Then it's time you go do something right. Go visit with Mary. Tell her how you're feeling."

"You don't think my visiting, or sharing my true feelings, will scare her off?"

"If she likes you at all, your visit will make her happy," she said, her expression melancholy. "Besides, John, if she likes you at all, she has been probably been thinking things that I have. Wondering why you aren't saying a thing . . ."

John watched Jayne leave. He was going to need to pay a call on Mary. Then and there, he was going to admit his feelings— and ask her some hard questions, too.

Such as if she only sought him out to help her son, or because she'd felt the same intangible bond that he did.

While planning his next step, and

watching Jayne's car leave the parking lot, Corrine, Mattie, Loyal, and Graham exited the hospital's main entrance.

"John, sorry you had to wait so long," Loyal said as they approached. "I wanted to talk to Ella's doctor, but finding him took a while."

"It was no problem." He unlocked the truck and slid behind the wheel as the other three squeezed in beside him. "I needed some time to regroup."

As Loyal followed his gaze, he patted his shoulder. "I reckon we all did, *Onkle*."

"Mattie, only you would think Ella needed a completely fresh bedroom to sleep in," Graham chided two days later as he carried out a second basket of laundry to the front lawn. "I'm sure Ella would be perfectly fine with the sheets that were already on the bed. Didn't you say that no one had slept in that room for weeks?"

"Yes, but I wanted them to smell fresh."

"I'm sure they smelled just fine." He frowned for good measure. "All this is doing is taking up a lot of time."

Men! Mattie knew she could spend the next hour telling him about how important it was for her to have a fresh room for Ella to sleep in—and he still wouldn't understand.

But of course, she couldn't chide him. He was giving up his whole afternoon to help her.

Though . . . he hadn't needed to. "You didn't have to help, you know," Mattie replied as she bent into the basket and awkwardly pulled out a wet quilt. "I didn't ask you to help."

"Careful." With a jerk of his hand, Graham pulled the quilt from her hands, expertly shook it out, and then competently pinned it on the clothesline.

Mattie watched in a combination of amusement and surprise. "I didn't know you knew how to pin clothes on the line."

"It's not difficult," he snapped.

"I didn't say it was."

Gently pushing her to one side, he pulled out a blanket snapped it, and pinned it up, too. "My *mamm* only had three boys," he finally said. "No daughters—until Katie came along."

"I know that."

"Three boys equal a lot of laundry. And, well, there was no way either Calvin or

Loyal were going to be seen putting clothes on the line . . ."

"Not if their little brother could do the work?" she finished with a smile.

"That is exactly right."

"Graham, but you don't need to pin up laundry here." With every article he pinned up, his mood seemed to darken. What in the world was wrong with him?

"Yes, I do." A note of iron entered his voice as he grabbed yet another pillowcase from her hands. "Mattie, you shouldn't be doing any of this. You shouldn't be lifting these heavy things. You could hurt yourself."

"I'm all right now." And she was. Didn't he even notice how much better she was? "As a matter of fact, I'm fine."

Graham's eyes narrowed at that. But instead of arguing, he just kept working. "Anyway, like I said, I can put up laundry just fine." As she stood with her arms over her chest, watching him move down the line to hang up a white sheet, he added, "Though, I also said that I don't understand why you're doing so much work. It's just Ella."

"That's the kind of thing I don't like to hear."

"What thing?"

"That *just*-Ella thing. Graham, I'm afraid she's used to everyone treating her like an afterthought."

"Dorothy didn't. Dorothy treated her like Ella couldn't do a thing without her."

"That's not fair."

"You're right. I'm sorry."

"Anyway, she needs someone to fuss over her. She's been through a difficult time."

"She has," he agreed. "I'm glad she's going to be all right."

Picking up one last pillowcase, he neatly pinned the white cotton on the line, then picked up the basket and guided Mattie to a bench nearby. "Done."

She turned and smiled at the sight. Two full lines were loaded down with sheets, pillowcases, and her mother's beautiful star quilt. "It's so warm out here, everything will be dry in no time."

"It *is* hot." He took off his hat and wiped his brow with a handkerchief. Mattie was just about to offer him a glass of lemonade when he turned to her. "Let's go sit in the shade and relax for a moment."

"You have time?"

"To watch the fruits of our labor? Definitely."

"All right," she said agreeably. She wasn't in any hurry for Graham to leave, anyway. Besides the search for Ella, they'd been spending very little time together. Far less than when she'd been receiving chemotherapy treatments. Of course, she shouldn't have expected anything different. Lots of people had seen him squiring Jenna around town.

He obviously had a lot to occupy him these days.

They walked to the shade of an old oak tree. On one side of it, the branches hung low and wide, creating a wide spot to sit under in relative comfort.

Since the ground was hard and dry, Mattie sat right down on the ground and leaned back against the trunk. Graham sat beside her. With her feet tucked neatly next to her, Graham kicked his legs out.

Above them, a squirrel berated them for disturbing his tree. Mattie chuckled as they watched him scramble to another tree, leaving them in peace.

The September day was warm. Though she hated to admit it to anyone, Mattie of-

ten did look forward to a nap in the afternoon. Her body seemed to be using all
her excess energy to heal.

As the quiet settled in around them and
the warm rays of sunshine warmed her
skin, her eyes drifted closed.

After a few moments, Graham shifted
and wrapped an arm around her shoulder,
letting her lean into him. She yawned and
let her body relax.

Mattie wasn't sure how long they sat together, there on the ground, warm from
the sun, secure in Graham's embrace. Ten
minutes? One hour?

No matter what, it felt like too short a
time had passed before he spoke. "So . . .
what do you think about Loyal and Ella?"
he said softly. "Do you think they're as serious as they look?"

"I don't know."

"Come now. Tell me what you think."

As usual, their siblinglike conversations
rejuvenated her. "I think they're turning serious. They'd have to be. Otherwise, why
would he have been so frantic?"

"True."

"Now it's your turn to talk. You're Loyal's
brother. What does he tell you?"

"Nothing. Every time I ask, he shuts me up with a fierce stare."

"And you let that stop you?"

"Pick your battles, you know."

"Well, what does Calvin say? I doubt Loyal has the nerve to glare at him."

Graham grinned. "You're right about that. He wouldn't dare glare at our older brother." He paused. "Of course, even if they did share information, it doesn't necessarily mean that they'll tell me anything."

Enjoying their conversation, Mattie sat up and grinned. "But what does he tell you? Come on, now. Tell me some news, Graham."

"All right. Calvin thinks they're serious. He even thinks Loyal might ask her to marry him soon."

Learning that bit of information drew a warm thread of happiness through her. There was something to be said for a happy ending. "That's *wunderbaar!*"

"I suppose. I never imagined my brother falling in love with a girl like Ella."

"I don't think it's a strange combination. I think they suit."

"Perhaps. I know they both enjoy the

house and the land. Though, I always imagined Loyal with someone different."

"How so?"

"Someone more outgoing, for one."

"I suppose you have a point there. Loyal is so outgoing and Ella is . . ." She struggled for the words.

"Not," Graham said. "She's as shy and awkward as Loyal is outgoing and polished."

"Well, opposites do attract."

"They do." A secret smile appeared on his face, making Mattie suspicious.

"What are you thinking about? *Who* are you thinking about?"

He glanced her way, then right there before her eyes, Graham blushed. "Jenna Yoder."

Jenna. "So you two are still seeing each other?" Oh, she hoped she sounded calm and collected.

"Some." Bringing his legs up, he rested his arms on his knees. "We get along well," he murmured. "Actually, Jenna seems to like just about everything I do. Unlike some people," he said sarcastically.

"What is that supposed to mean? Are you talking about me?"

"Obviously. You'd say the sky was green if I called it blue."

Stung, she got to her feet. "That's not true."

Grinning, he stood as well. "Perhaps not strictly true. But you have to admit, Mattie Lapp, we spar more than any two people I've ever met."

"It's all in fun."

"Yes. But thank goodness we aren't interested in each other."

She blinked. "Yes. Thank goodness."

Just as quickly as it had come, his teasing grin vanished. In its place was a speculative glance. Making her feel like he was reading her mind.

What was he thinking? Did he, too, think that there was more to the two of them than they'd ever imagined?

Of course, it didn't matter.

"The laundry will be dry soon," she murmured.

He stepped backward. "Yes. Then you don't need me anymore."

She needed him in her life, but that couldn't happen. "*Nee*. I don't need you . . . for the laundry."

"Then I'll be on my way." His gaze gentled for a moment. He raised his hand. For a split second, she was sure he was going to run his fingers along her cheek.

But of course he did not.

"Goodbye, Graham. I'll see you later."

"Yes. Goodbye, Mattie."

As Mattie watched him leave, she had the sudden feeling that they were saying goodbye to far more than just the day.

Chapter 30

"Ella, do you feel like having some visitors?" Mattie asked. "Loyal and Katie are out on the front porch."

"They're here to see me?"

"Of course."

Ella smoothed her dress and apron around her legs and lap. Just this morning, Mattie had helped her dress; and though the process of getting dressed with a hurt collarbone and a cast on her leg had been exhausting, the results had been worth it.

Now, at least, she felt more like herself. Over the last two days, her wounds were still hurting, but the worst of the pain had definitely abated. "Do I look okay?"

"You look great. Much better," Mattie promised. "Now you sit still and I'll go bring them in here."

Ella watched from her spot on the couch. The moment Mattie approached the screen door, Loyal opened it from the other side. After greeting her, he sauntered into the *sitzschtupp*. "Ella, hello."

As usual, his smile was sunny and perfect.

Leaving Ella feeling even more aware of her scars and injuries. "Hello. And hello to you, too, Katie dear."

Wary, Katie edged forward far behind Loyal. When she was a full two feet away, she stopped, her eyes wide.

"Katie, does the bandage on my head scare you?"

After a hesitation, Katie nodded. "And the others, too. You've got cuts on your face."

"I know." Lifting up the hem of her dress a bit, she said, "And I have a pink cast."

"I've been sad about you," Katie stated, then stepped closer, her hand out.

"*Nee*, Katie," Loyal said.

But Ella knew what Katie had in mind. "Did you want to touch my cast?"

"Uh-huh."

"You may rub it gently, if you want. It feels rough, *jah*?"

After rubbing her hand along a good six inches of Ella's cast, Katie looked at her and smiled.

Sharing a smile with Loyal, Ella said, "Seeing you here makes me happy. I'm glad you came to visit."

Katie skipped back to the front door, bent down to picked something up, then returned with a wrapped package. "Ella, we have a present for you."

"You do? *Danke*." Smiling at both of them, she turned the brightly wrapped box over in her hands. It was rather big, about the size of a puzzle box. But heavier.

What in the world could it be?

She shook it again, enjoying the expectation almost as much as a child would. It had been quite a while since someone had given her such a fancily wrapped package.

But Katie, obviously, was having none of those same feelings. "Don't'cha want to open it?"

Beside her, Loyal pressed one firm hand to her shoulder. "Katie. Mind your manners. This isn't about what you want, remember?"

"Sorry," she said.

"I don't mind your excitement at all. Come here and sit with me and help, would you?" Ella saw her hands were trembling slightly. A little embarrassed about that, she put the package down on her lap but motioned Katie closer. "All this paper might be too much for me. Do you think you could help?"

"Uh-huh." When Loyal's hand dropped, she edged closer to Ella. Her eyes were shining with happiness, making Ella's heart expand. Oh, she did so love children, and Katie especially.

"Here you go," Ella said, handing the package to Katie. "Help me unwrap."

"You're going to love it," Katie blurted, breaking the tape and ripping the wrapping paper with great enthusiasm. A three-inch line of paper fell onto the wood floor.

Ella laughed.

But Loyal sighed. "Careful now, Katie," he warned.

When the paper was completely off,

Loyal placed the box back on Ella's lap. "It's your turn to open the present now."

Ella followed directions, lifting the cardboard lid and handing it to Katie. Next, she opened the tissue covering.

And then she stilled, her eyes filling with tears. "Oh, my," she said. "It's *schee*! Beautiful."

"Take it out, yes?"

Carefully, she took out the large square wooden box, finely made out of oak and stained a rich, deep brown. Hinges were on one side. She opened the lid, enjoying how the hinge was so smooth. The inside was lined with dark green velvet.

"It's a memory box," Loyal said, his expression kind. "I saw it and thought of you." He shrugged. "And, of course, the Bible verse made me think of you."

She ran a finger along the words engraved into the wood. "*Now faith is being sure of what we hope for and certain of what we do not see,*" she read. A little tremor went through her. It was as if Loyal had read her mind and then inscribed the words onto the lid of the box.

Beside her, Katie ran her finger along the writing, too. Then, seemingly satisfied that their gift was liked, she left them. Behind them, the door opened and shut, followed by Katie's chatter to Mattie and her parents.

Now they were completely alone. And Ella wished she had better control of her emotions. Tears threatened to fall, and her emotions were so high, she was almost afraid to speak.

But of course she needed to.

"This verse, it means so much," she said, trying to describe her feelings. "These past few months, with my mother passing and then selling the farm, and finally everything going on with Dorothy . . . I've never felt more alone." She looked at Loyal, hoping there was a way she could make him understand what was deep inside her soul. "But I've also never felt so close with the Lord. It's like he's been talking with me, holding me up, giving me strength."

"That's what faith is, yes? The certainty that the impossible can happen?"

Ella looked at him in wonder. Never would she have imagined that Loyal ever thought like that. He seemed so grounded, so surrounded by the love of his family. Though she knew he believed in God, of course, she hadn't imagined that he would have relied on faith, too.

"Yes," she finally answered. "That is what faith is to me. It means believing in our Lord, no matter what." Though she knew no words could adequately convey the strong emotions building inside of her, she tried her best. "I truly do thank you for this."

"I'm glad you like it. I thought, maybe, you would like to start putting some of your special things inside it." His eyes darkened. "I know you still regret selling so much at the auction."

She shook her head. "I don't," she protested. "Not anymore. It was all just *stuff*. The memories are what I will cherish. Though, I have to admit that I will enjoy keeping special things in this in the future."

Suddenly, she felt like they were too close. After carefully setting the keepsake box back in the cardboard container, she scooted a few inches away.

Loyal stood up.

Looking up at him, she suddenly had the urge to stand by his side. "Could you help me stand for a moment?" she whispered.

"Ella, I don't think that's wise."

"I've used crutches to get to this room. It would be nice to be on my feet, at least for a few moments."

Looking as if he could deny her nothing, Loyal bent and grasped her waist. With her arms on his shoulders and her good foot on the ground, she pushed herself upright.

"Better?" Loyal murmured, his hands still at her waist.

"Better." Liking the feel of him, she kept one hand on his shoulder, the other on his bicep.

When he looked down at her, his gaze gentle, Ella relaxed. Standing there beside him, she didn't feel too tall at all. As a matter of fact, they were compatible in many ways. He was only a few inches taller than she.

And he was a large man. His shoulders were wide—far wider than hers. All of him was much bigger. Making her think for the first time that maybe she didn't need to have another woman's petite beauty to garner a handsome, good man's attention. Maybe she didn't need perfect eyesight. Or bright blue eyes.

Or a sparkling, fiery personality.

For Loyal Weaver, maybe she only had to be herself.

Swallowing, she met his gaze again. What she saw there made her heart melt. There was complete acceptance there, even though at the moment she had cuts on her face and hands and bruises all over. With one hand, he trailed a path down her arm, finally coming to a stop on the top of her hand. With a featherlight touch, he traced a path over her knuckle.

"Ella, when you are feeling better, I'd like you to come over. To the farm."

"I'd like that. I can't wait to see what other improvements you've made."

"I'll be glad to show you everything I've been working on," he said quietly as he reached out and brushed two fingers along her cheek. "But, really, I want you to come over because I want to be alone with you."

With effort, she contained her surprise. Loyal looked troubled and earnest all at the same time. What a funny combination! "Well, I'll look forward to it." Though every muscle in her body ached, she straightened a bit. "I'm sure I will feel better soon."

Loyal turned, carefully rested both of his

hands at her waist. His grip was secure, making sure she didn't fall. But tender, too.

She felt guarded by his arms. Protected. Clumsily, she raised her other hand so both rested on his shoulders. In a rush, she felt heat flood into her cheeks. Never before had she been held like this.

And goodness, it wasn't even really an embrace. She didn't know what it was.

Loyal smiled. "This is nice."

"*Jah*. I mean, it is."

To her surprise, he leaned a small bit closer. Just moving those three inches changed things considerably. Now his whole palm instead of his fingertips curved around her waist.

Now her wrists lay on his chest. She swallowed.

His gaze darkened. "One day, Ella . . ." he murmured. "One day maybe we'll stand together."

What was he talking about?

Afraid to ask and spoil the moment, Ella said nothing, simply stared at him . . . before closing her eyes as he leaned closer and brushed his lips against her cheek.

He stepped away in a rush. Dropped his hands. "I had best collect Katie and leave you."

"You don't have to—"

"I had better." Almost sheepishly he looked at her again before helping her back to her seat. "I'll visit you again tomorrow."

"All right," she said helplessly. Picking up the box, she looked at the engraving in the wood while he went to retrieve his sister. Then she watched them walk out of the house.

Mattie followed them out to the porch, stood next to Loyal and Katie and said goodbye as they walked toward the path.

When they were completely alone, Ella looked at the box and then at Mattie. "I'm not quite sure what just happened."

Crouching in front of her, Mattie admired the gift. "What did happen?" she asked with a smile.

"Loyal gave me this. Said it reminded him of me. And then we stood together." She tried to think of a way to describe their embrace that wasn't really one.

To describe his kiss that was truly noth- ing more than a brief brush of his lips against her cheek. But no descriptor seemed appropriate.

Finally, she gave up. "I don't know how to describe it. It was just . . . nice." She frowned. Nice certainly wasn't the correct way to describe how she felt . . . how blue Loyal's eyes were.

But Mattie just looked at the box, then at her . . . in a dreamy way. "Oh, Ella. It sounds perfect."

"It was perfect."

Mattie laughed. "Come now, it's time for you to go lie down."

"Oh, I couldn't—"

Mattie laughed again. "Oh, Ella. If you could see yourself."

"Do I look awful?"

She shook her head. "*Nee*. Ella, you look happy. So very happy."

And that, Ella realized, was true. She was happy. Completely at peace.

She'd almost forgotten what that had felt like.

Chapter 31

September 17, 2:00 P.M.

Loyal came over the next day. And the next. And the day after that. Each time, he came alone—and each time, Ella felt a little more breathless when he left.

Although nothing had been said, of course, Loyal seemed to be endlessly giving her hints about his heart. And about their future together.

On the fourth day he came calling, Ella greeted him in her favorite dark blue dress.

"Look at you," he said with a smile. "You look so pretty, one would hardly know you've got a cast on your leg."

She laughed. "I finally feel better. More myself, I think." She gestured to the pitcher of iced tea next to her. "Maybe you'd like something to drink?"

"Sure." He stood awkwardly next to her for a moment, then leaned down and helped her pour. Before she sipped her own, he set the glass down. "Ella, I've been waiting for a perfect time, but the fact is, I'm too nervous."

"Why in the world would you be nervous?"

Taking her hand in his, he said, "Because I want to ask you to marry me."

"Want to? Or you are going to?"

His cheeks flushed. Looking remarkably unsure, he rubbed the pad of his thumb across her knuckle. "I want to," he said, flashing an embarrassed smile. After taking a breath, he lifted his chin. "Will you marry me, Ella? Will you live with me on the farm that's been in your family for generations—and start your own family with me?"

Ella knew if she'd tried for a thousand days, she could have never asked for a sweeter question. Right then and there,

Loyal was giving her everything she'd always wanted. A man to love. A family to cherish.

And a life that she could wake up each morning and smile about.

"Of course," she said simply.

His answering smile was beautiful. His gentle embrace was perfect.

And his kiss, well, his kiss was everything she'd ever dreamed about . . . when she'd been sitting alone on a bench in her yard . . . hoping one day to have the life she'd always wanted.

Dear Reader,

Thank you for reading my book! I hope you are enjoying this series and were rooting for Ella to find both love and happiness as much as I was.

When I began this novel, I wavered back and forth about whether to put Katie's point of view in it. In the end, I decided to include it because I really could identify with her love of reading. I was never very precocious—I was way too shy for that—but I could definitely relate to Katie's eagerness to be in the summer reading club. Maybe some of you have also participated in that a time or two?

This letter wouldn't be complete without offering my thanks to many people. First and foremost, I'm so thankful to my husband, Tom. Tom, I could never write so much without your help and support. Thank you for listening for hours about made-up people, and for cooking and cleaning that kitchen!

Thank you, also, to my critique partners, Heather, Cathy, Hilda, and Tonya. For over ten years now, we've met and eaten donuts and sipped coffee and laughed. What would I do without y'all? Thanks for quickly reading chapters, giving me encouragement, and letting me know when I've really messed things up. I never take your advice, your help, or your friendship for granted.

Thank you also needs to go to my editor, Cindy DiTiberio. Thank you, Cindy, for making so many of my dreams possible—and for letting me follow the characters where they want to go . . . even when the novels aren't *quite* like I proposed. Because of you, writing is still so very fun.

And, finally, thank you to all of the readers who've reached out to me in countless ways. Thank you for coming to book signings, for asking your librarians to order copies of my novels, and for giving my books as gifts.

Thanks for finding me on Facebook and for visiting my Web site. Thank you for your prayers and your kind words and your encouragement. I'm forever grateful for your support.

With His blessings and my thanks,

Shelley

Book Discussion Questions

1. Ella and Loyal have lived near each other for most of their lives, but until recently, hardly knew each other at all. Have you ever had a relationship like that with someone? How did your relationship grow and change?

2. Should Loyal have felt guilty for purchasing the Hostetler farm? Or was the purchase the right thing for both Ella and him?

3. The practice of auctioning off a deceased person's belongings is a

common practice in some Amish communities. Many Amish feel it is best to honor memories, not mementoes. How do you feel about this practice? Are there some things you've inherited that you could do without? Is there anything that you could never part with?

4. The theme of friendship plays an important part in the novel. Ella learns she must reach out to people in order for them to reach out to her. How have friends played a role in your life? What makes someone a good friend to you?

5. Dorothy, of course, exemplifies everything friendship is not. She's self-serving and possessive, which leads to her downfall. How do you think she could have changed throughout the book? Or do you think her fate was inevitable?

6. Loyal, being the middle son, is trying hard to find his independence. Do you think his purchasing the Hostetler farm was the right decision? What other problems might a middle child face, even as an adult?

7. In *The Protector,* John Weaver is still struggling with his future. Do you think he could have been happy with Jayne Donovan, and staying "English"?

8. The main storylines in the novel revolve around "protecting" something, whether it is a reputation, a friendship, a future, or a love. Some of the characters risk almost everything they have for these things. What would you go to great lengths to protect? Why?

9. The Bible verse that guided me while writing *The Protector* was from Hebrews: "Now faith is being sure of what we hope for and certain of what we do not see." —Hebrews 11:1 (NIV*)* What does faith mean to you? How does your faith play a role in your daily life?

10. How might the following Amish proverb apply to you? What does "sharing your joys" look like in your life?

Share your joys with others. It takes two to be glad.

Shelley Shepard Gray

Mary Lou Zinsser

SHELLEY SHEPARD GRAY is the beloved author of the Seasons of Sugarcreek series as well as the Sisters of the Heart series, including *Hidden*, *Wanted*, and *Forgiven*. Before writing, she was a teacher in both Texas and Colorado. She now writes full-time and lives in southern Ohio with her husband and two children. When not writing, Shelley volunteers at church, reads, and enjoys walking her miniature dachshund on her town's scenic bike trail.